ROBIN HOOD

retold by Aaron Shepard and Anne L. Watson
illustrated by Jennifer Tanner

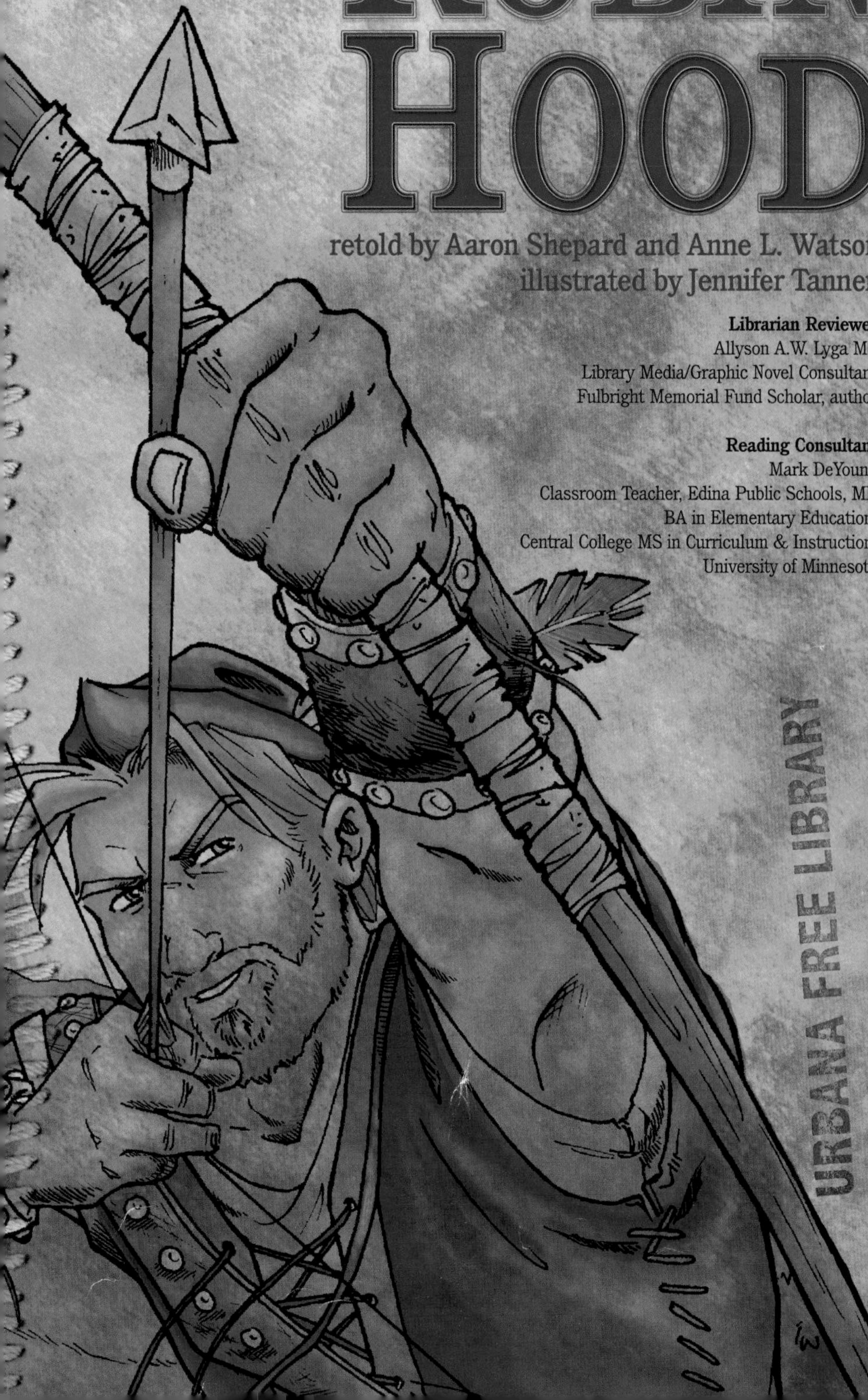

Librarian Reviewer
Allyson A.W. Lyga MS
Library Media/Graphic Novel Consultant
Fulbright Memorial Fund Scholar, author

Reading Consultant
Mark DeYoung
Classroom Teacher, Edina Public Schools, MN
BA in Elementary Education,
Central College MS in Curriculum & Instruction,
University of Minnesota

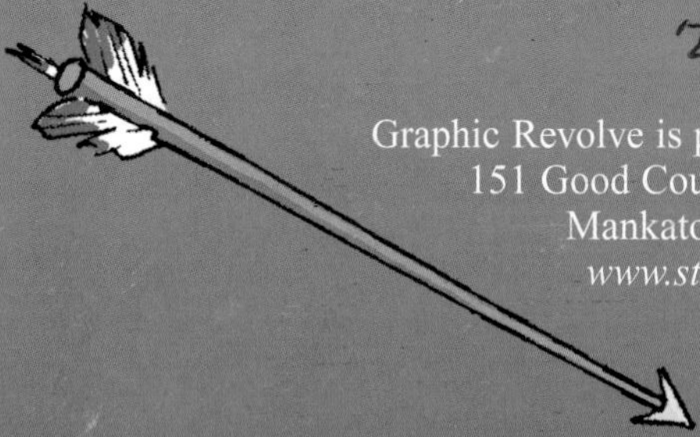

Graphic Revolve is published by Stone Arch Books,
151 Good Counsel Drive, P.O. Box 669,
Mankato, Minnesota 56002.
www.stonearchbooks.com

Library of Congress Cataloging-in-Publication Data
Shepard, Aaron.
Robin Hood / retold by Aaron Shepard and Anne L. Watson; illustrated by Jennifer Tanner.
p. cm.—(Graphic Revolve)
ISBN-13: 978-1-59889-049-5 (hardcover)
ISBN-10: 1-59889-049-2 (hardcover)
ISBN-13: 978-1-59889-219-2 (paperback)
ISBN-10: 1-59889-219-3 (paperback)
1. Graphic novels. I. Watson, Anne L. II. Tanner, Jennifer. III. Robin Hood (Legend). English. IV. Title. V. Series.
PN6727.S497R63 2007
741.5'973—dc22 2006007694

Summary: Robin Hood and his band of outlaws are the heroes of Sherwood Forest. Taking from the rich and giving to the poor, Robin Hood and his loyal followers fight for the oppressed and against the evil Sheriff of Nottingham.

Credits
Art Director: Heather Kindseth
Graphic Designer: Kay Fraser

1 2 3 4 5 6 11 10 09 08 07 06

Printed in the United States of America

Table of Contents

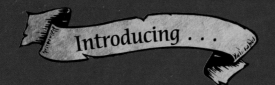
Introducing . . .

Robin Hood
A bold young outlaw

Marian
Robin's love

Will Scarlet
Robin's cousin

Little John
Robin's right-hand man

Edward and Sir Stephen
Eleanor's father and his chosen groom

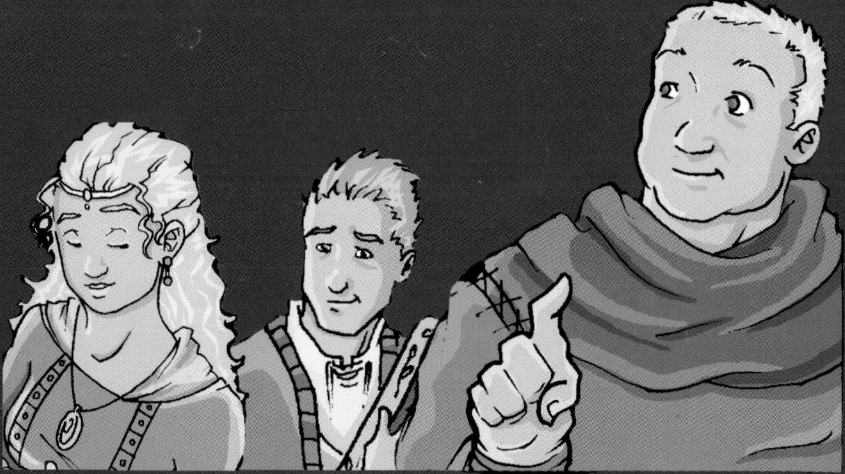

Eleanor and Alan-a-Dale
A wandering minstrel and his love

Friar Tuck
A wandering monk

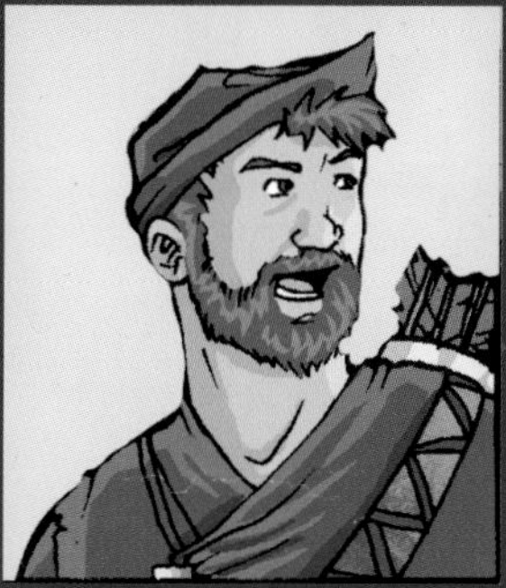

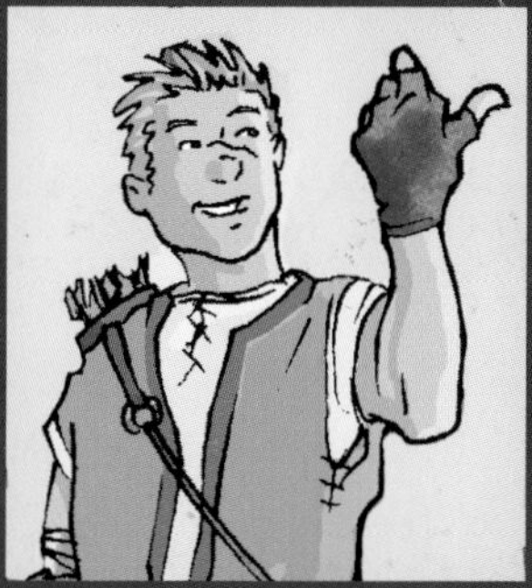

David of Doncaster and Will Stutely
Other men of Robin's band

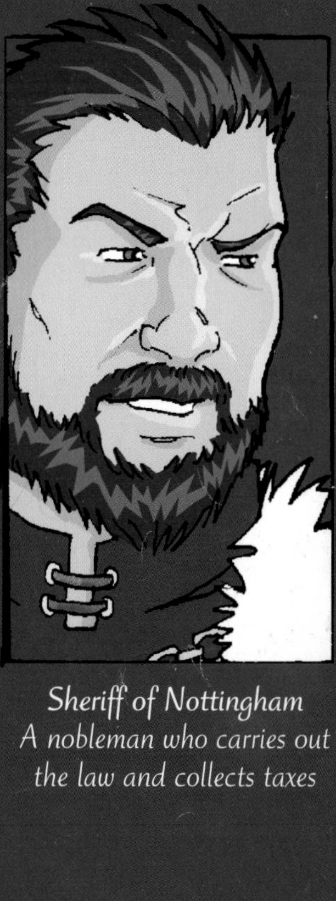

Sheriff of Nottingham
A nobleman who carries out the law and collects taxes

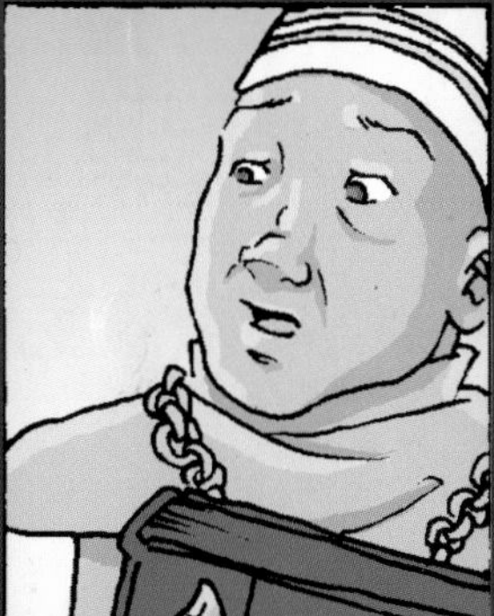

Bishop of Hereford
A man of the Church

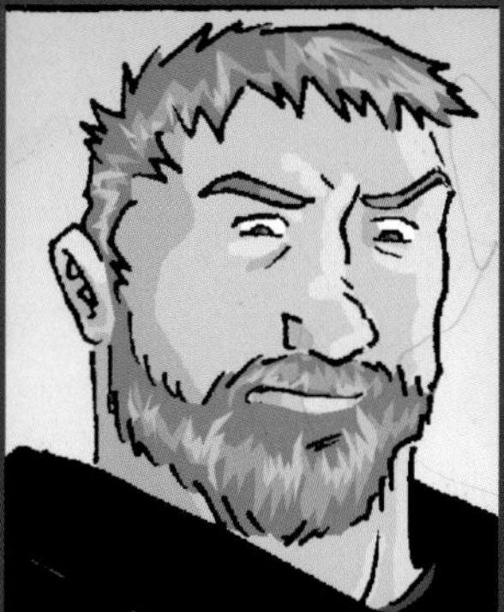

King Richard
Ruler of England from 1189 to 1199

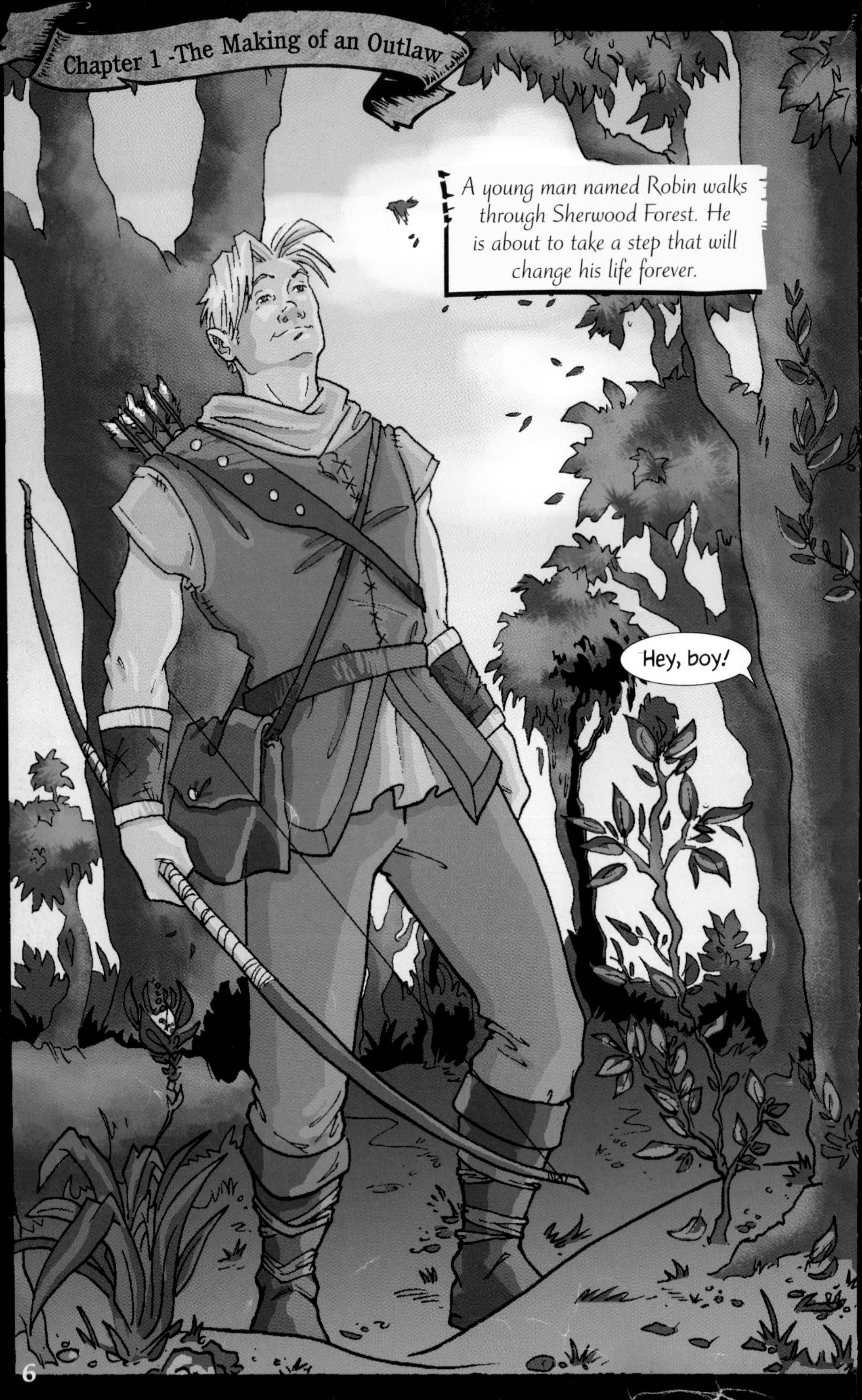
Chapter 1 -The Making of an Outlaw
A young man named Robin walks through Sherwood Forest. He is about to take a step that will change his life forever.
Hey, boy!

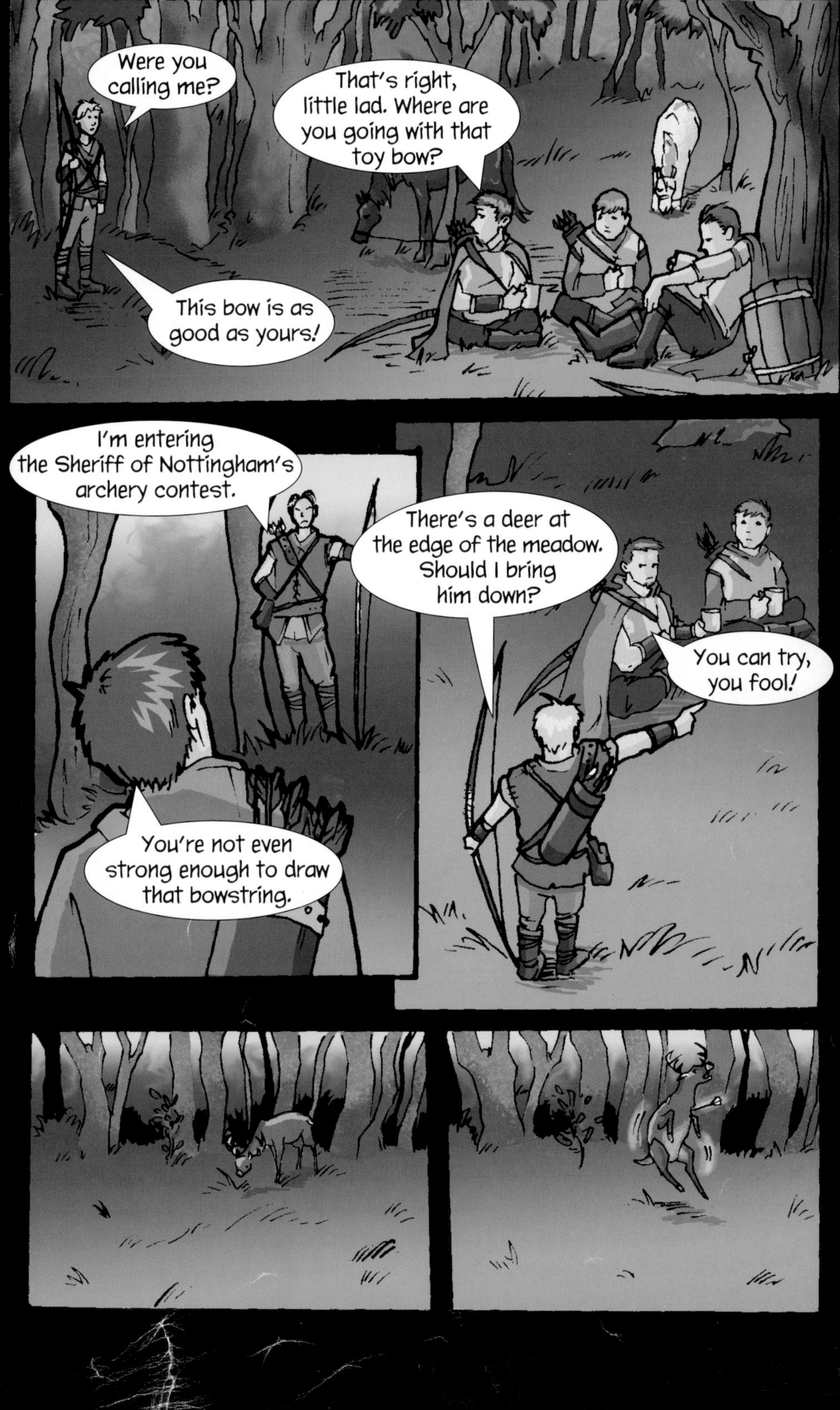
Were you calling me?
That's right, little lad. Where are you going with that toy bow?
This bow is as good as yours!
I'm entering the Sheriff of Nottingham's archery contest.
You're not even strong enough to draw that bowstring.
There's a deer at the edge of the meadow. Should I bring him down?
You can try, you fool!

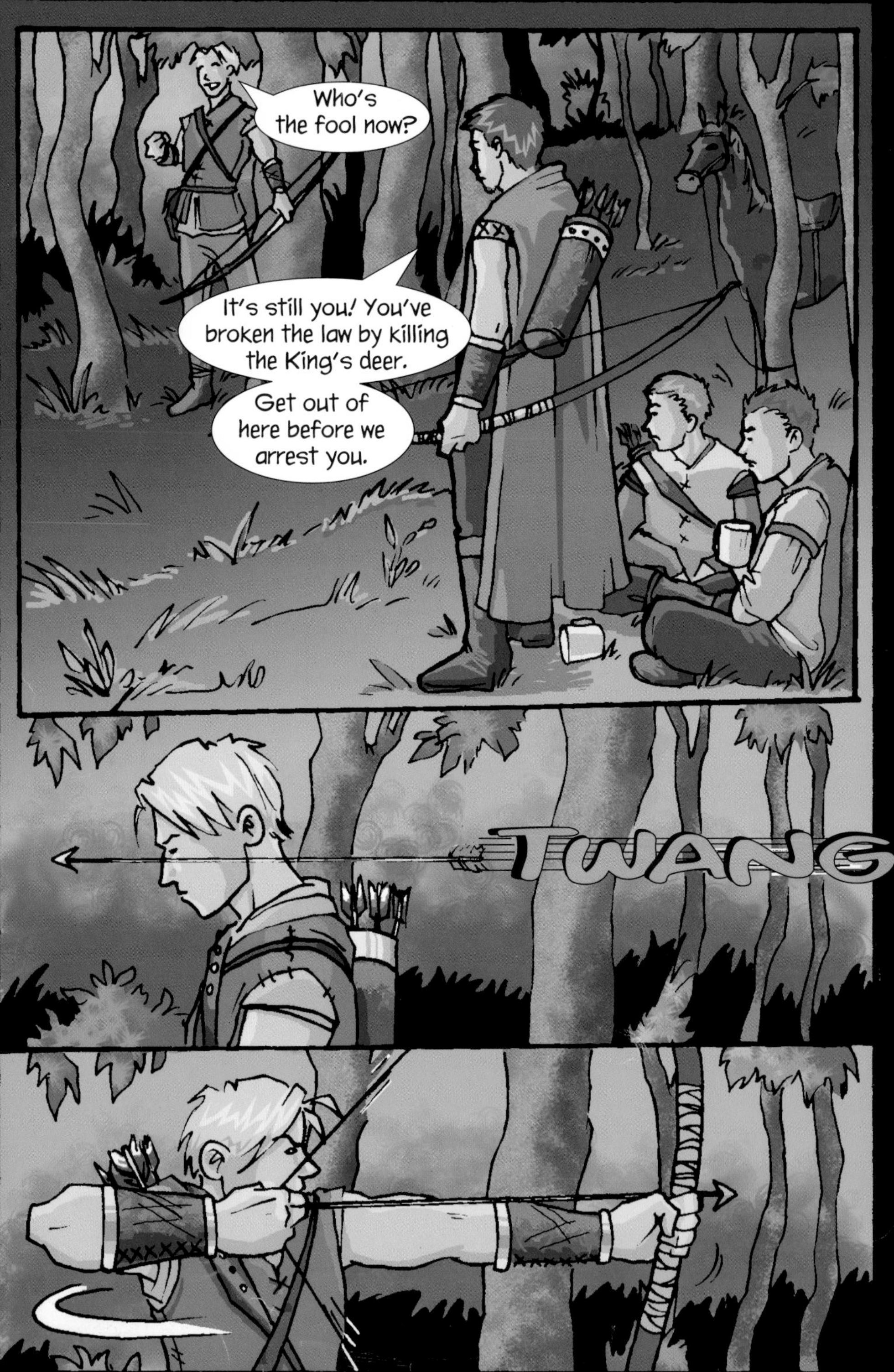
Who's the fool now?
It's still you! You've broken the law by killing the King's deer.
Get out of here before we arrest you.
TWANG

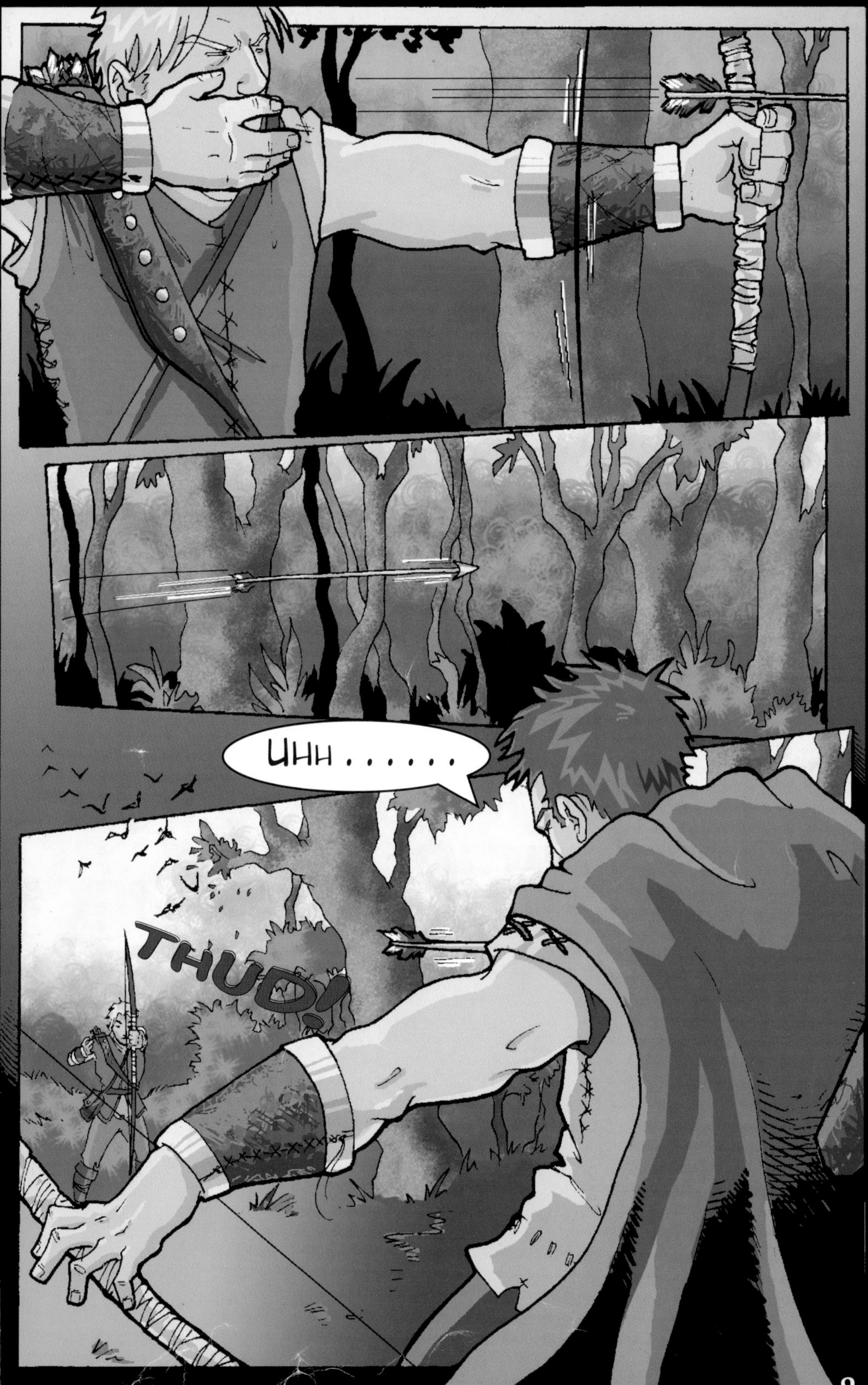
UHH . . . . . .
THUD!

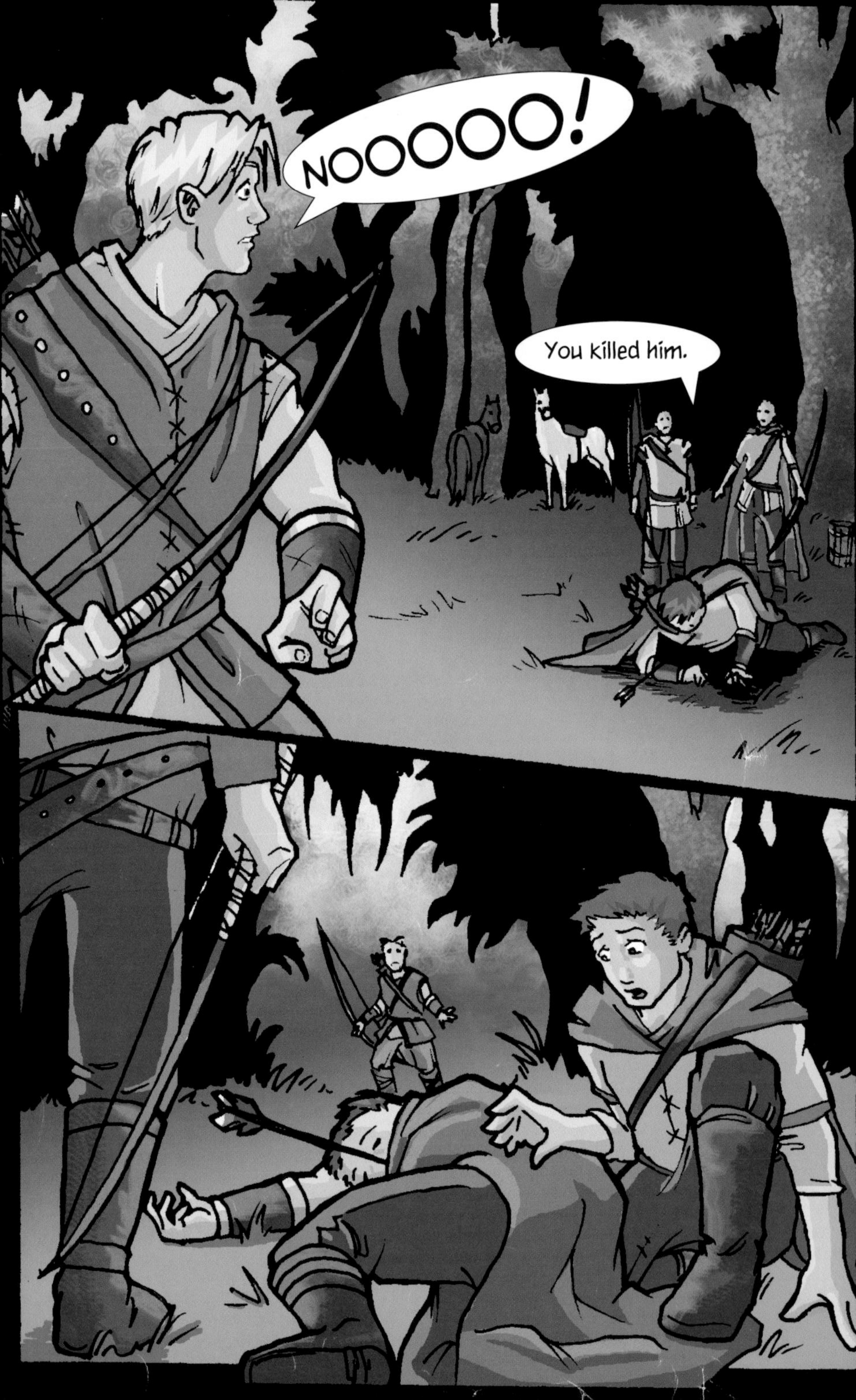
NOOOOO!
You killed him.

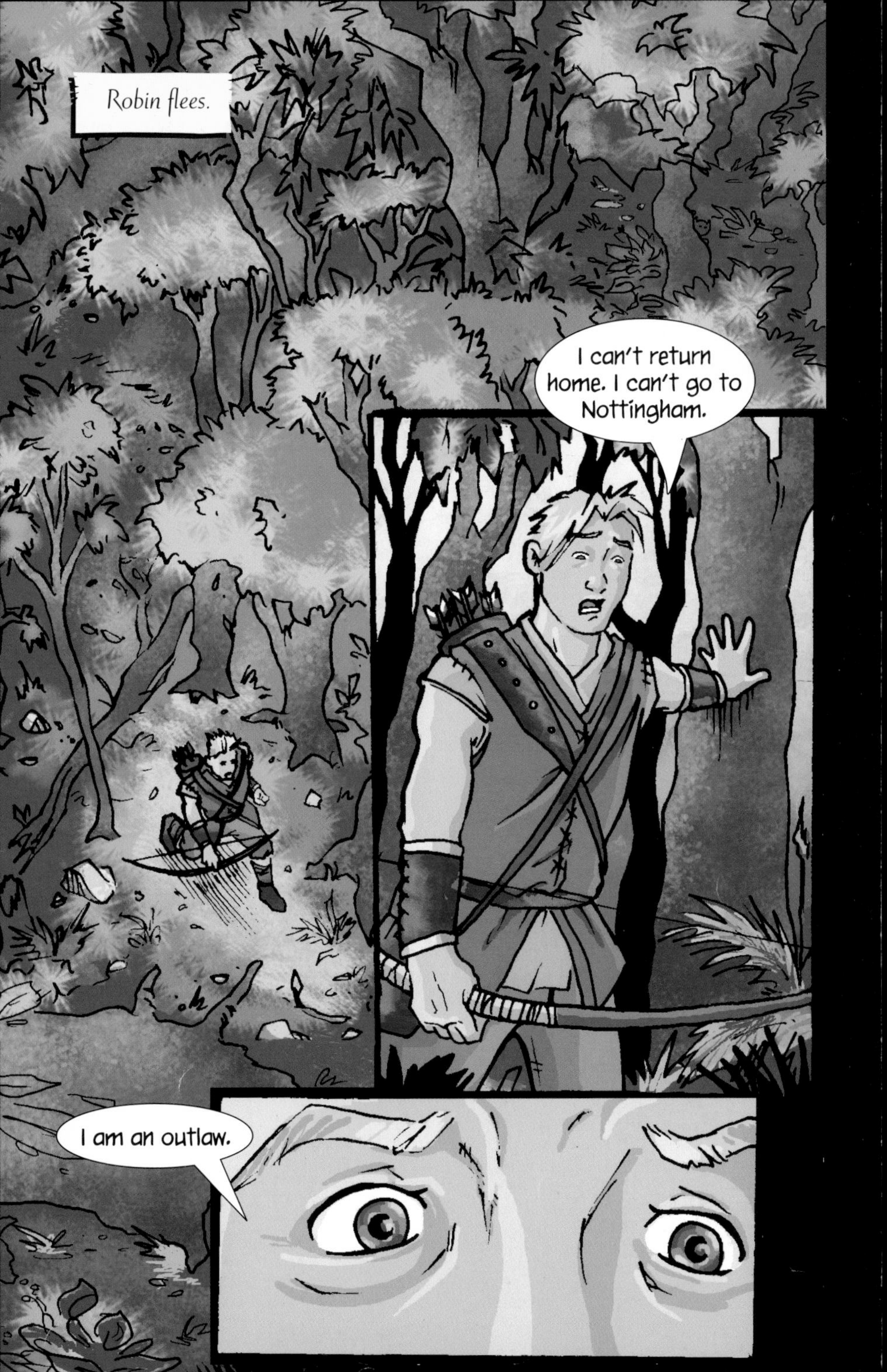
Robin flees.
I can't return home. I can't go to Nottingham.
I am an outlaw.

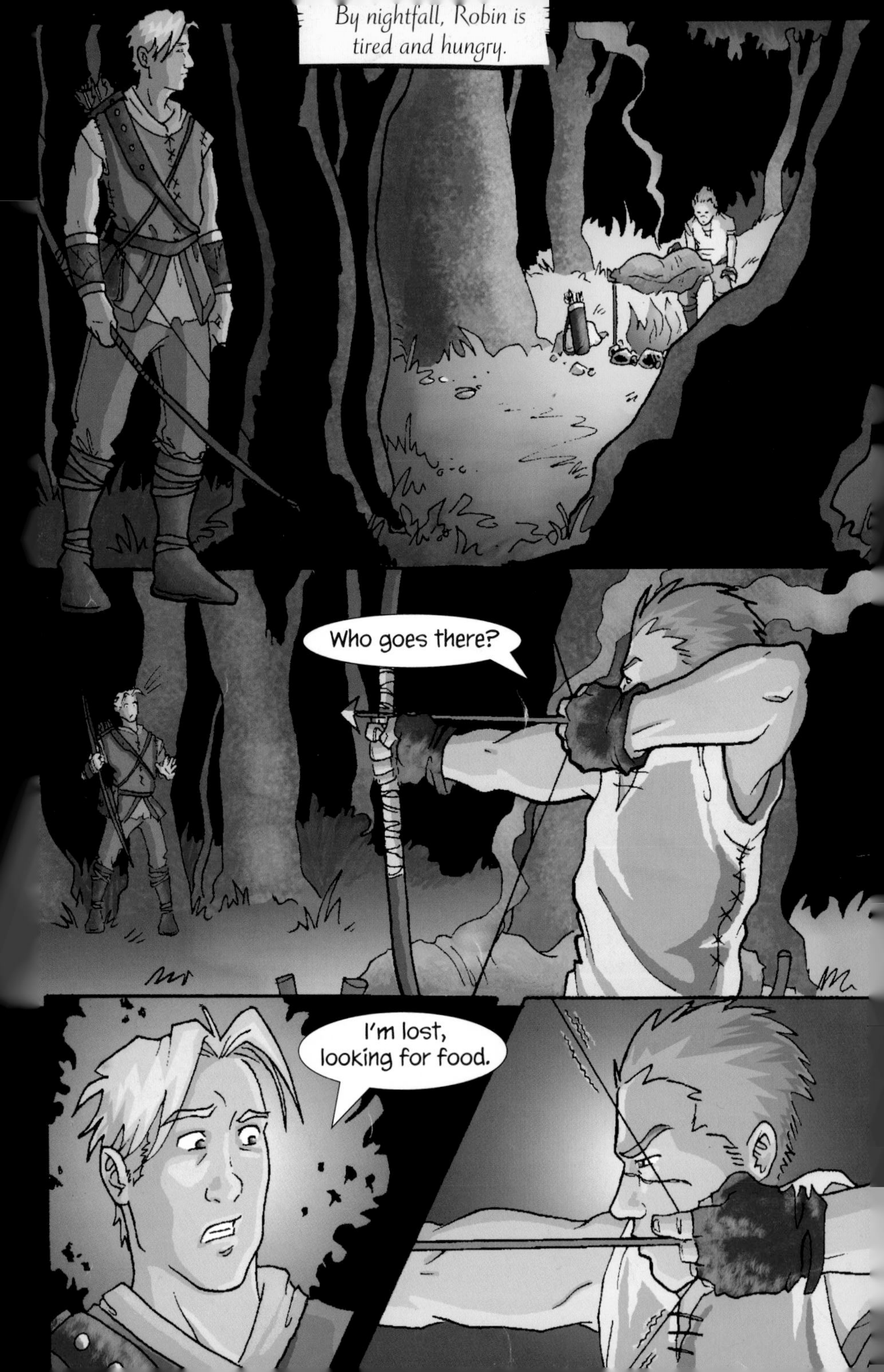
By nightfall, Robin is tired and hungry.
Who goes there?
I'm lost, looking for food.

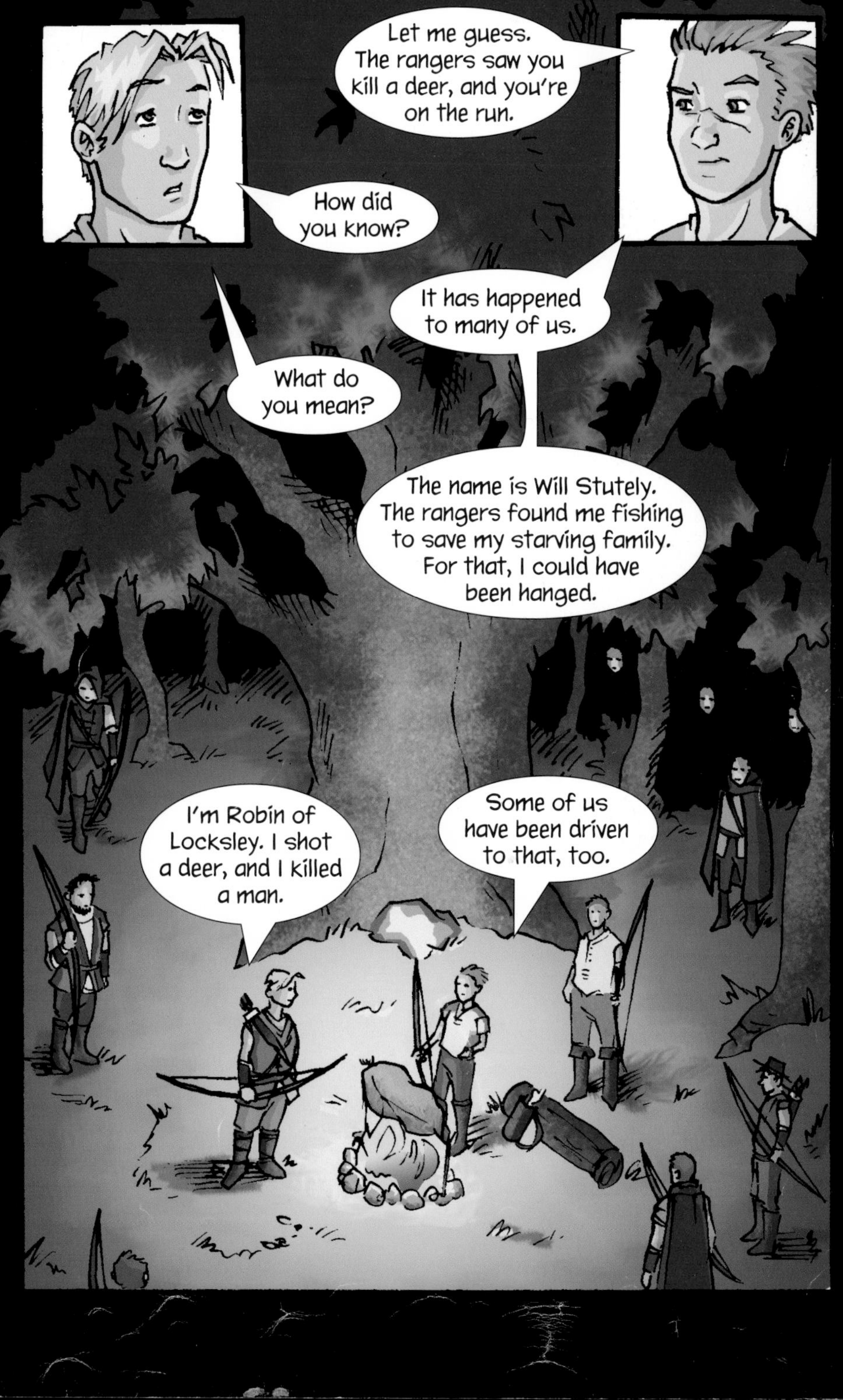
Let me guess. The rangers saw you kill a deer, and you're on the run.
How did you know?
It has happened to many of us.
What do you mean?
The name is Will Stutely. The rangers found me fishing to save my starving family. For that, I could have been hanged.
I'm Robin of Locksley. I shot a deer, and I killed a man.
Some of us have been driven to that, too.

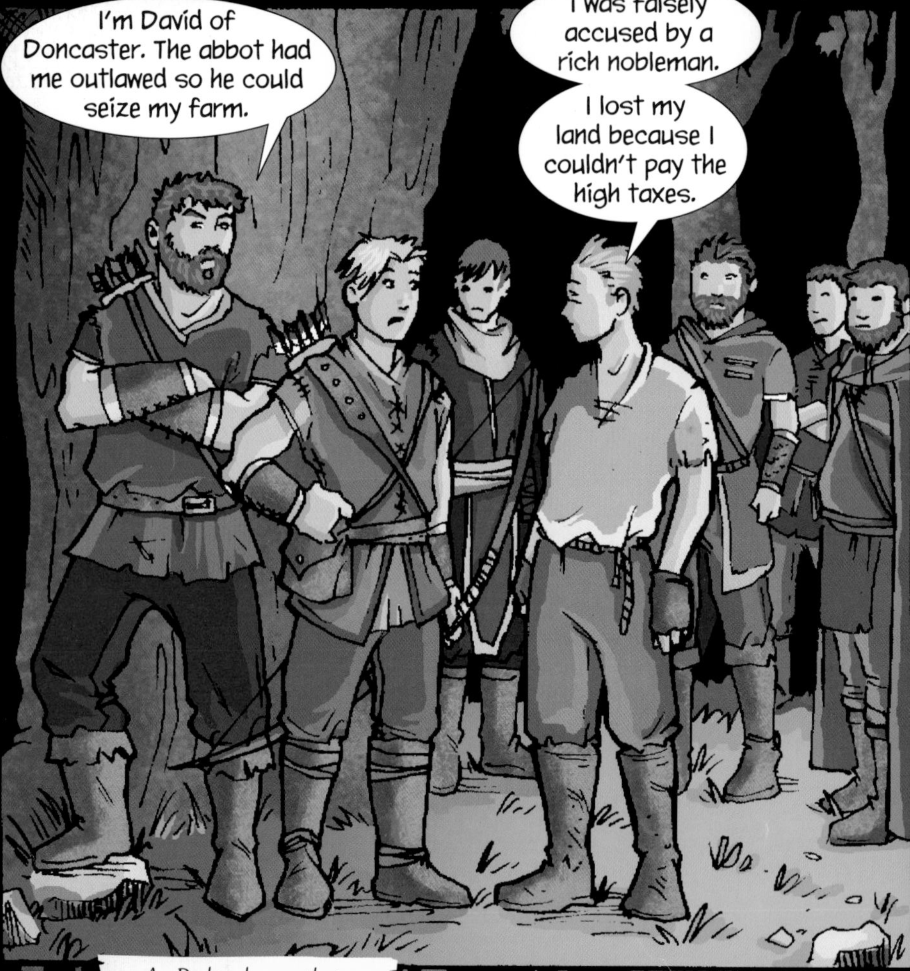

I'm David of Doncaster. The abbot had me outlawed so he could seize my farm.
I was falsely accused by a rich nobleman.
I lost my land because I couldn't pay the high taxes.

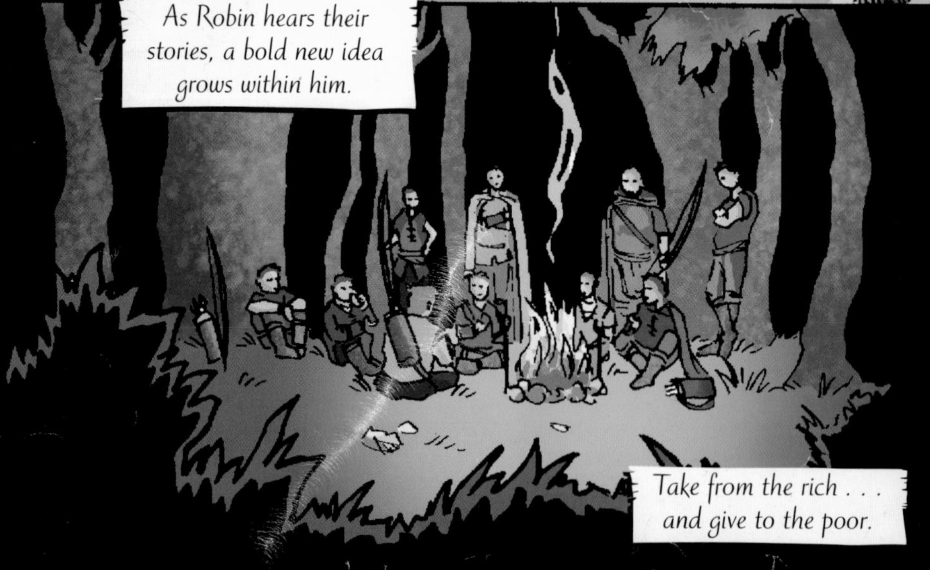

As Robin hears their stories, a bold new idea grows within him.
Take from the rich . . . and give to the poor.

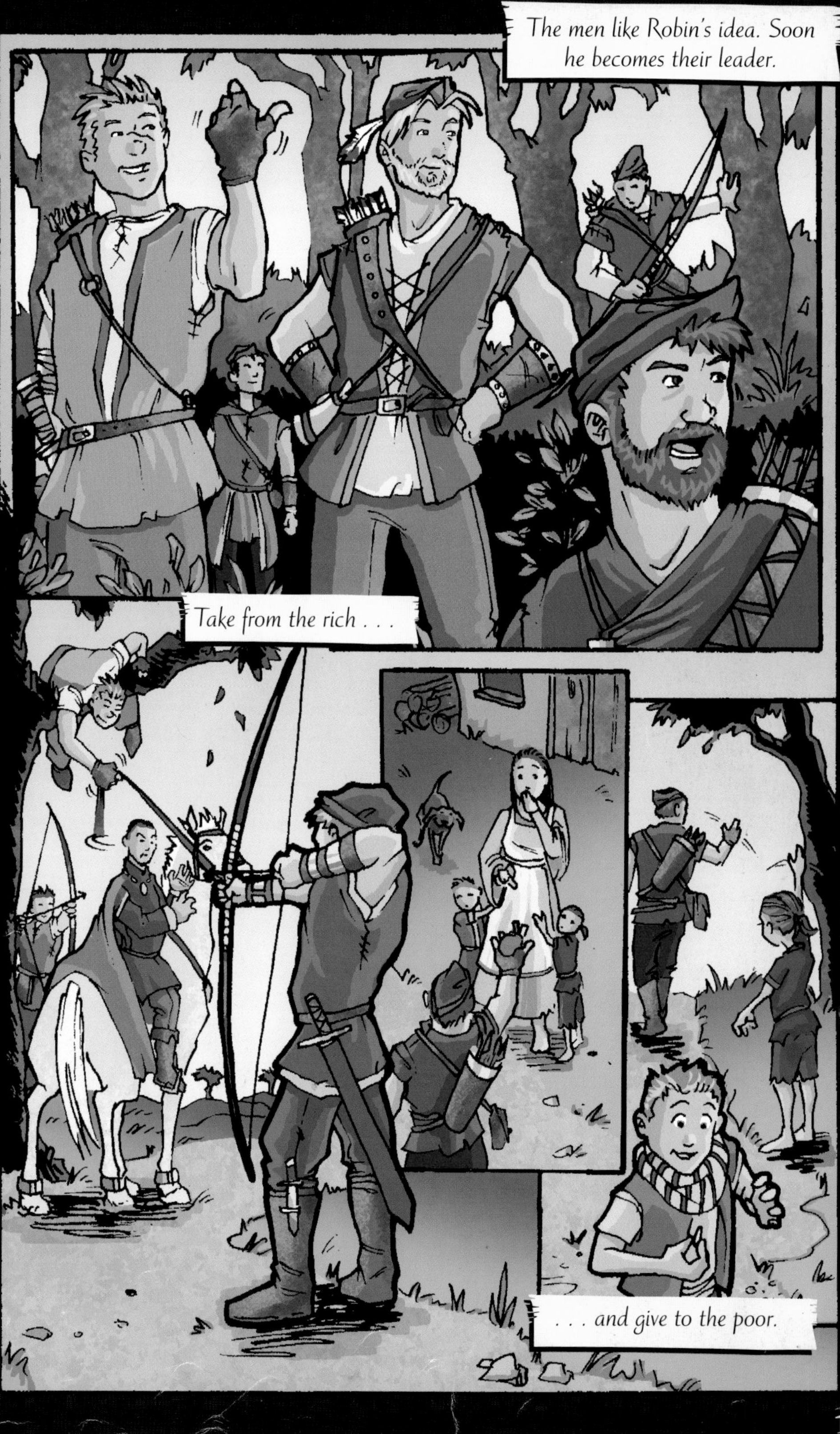
The men like Robin's idea. Soon he becomes their leader.
Take from the rich . . .
. . . and give to the poor.

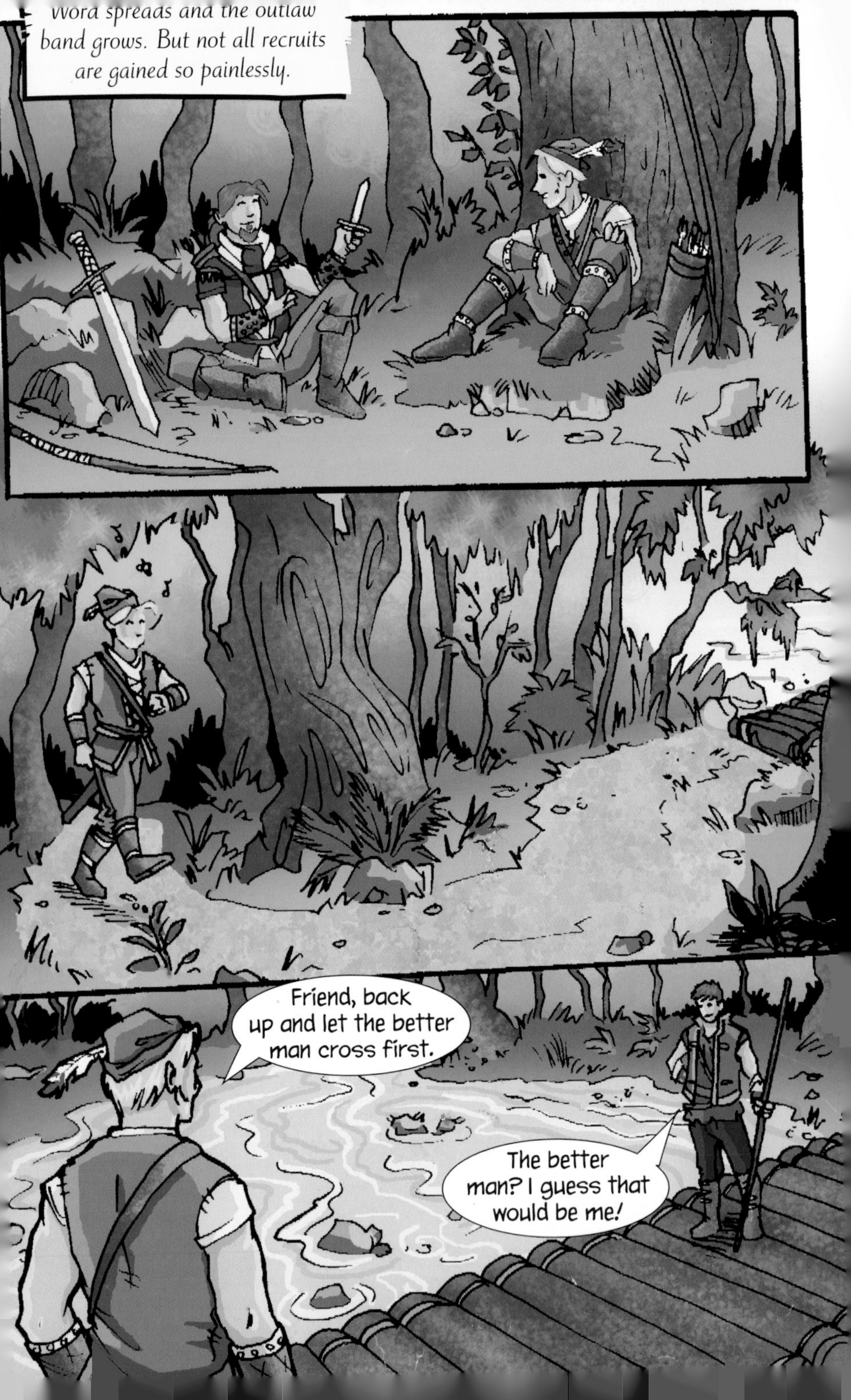
Word spreads and the outlaw band grows. But not all recruits are gained so painlessly.
Friend, back up and let the better man cross first.
The better man? I guess that would be me!

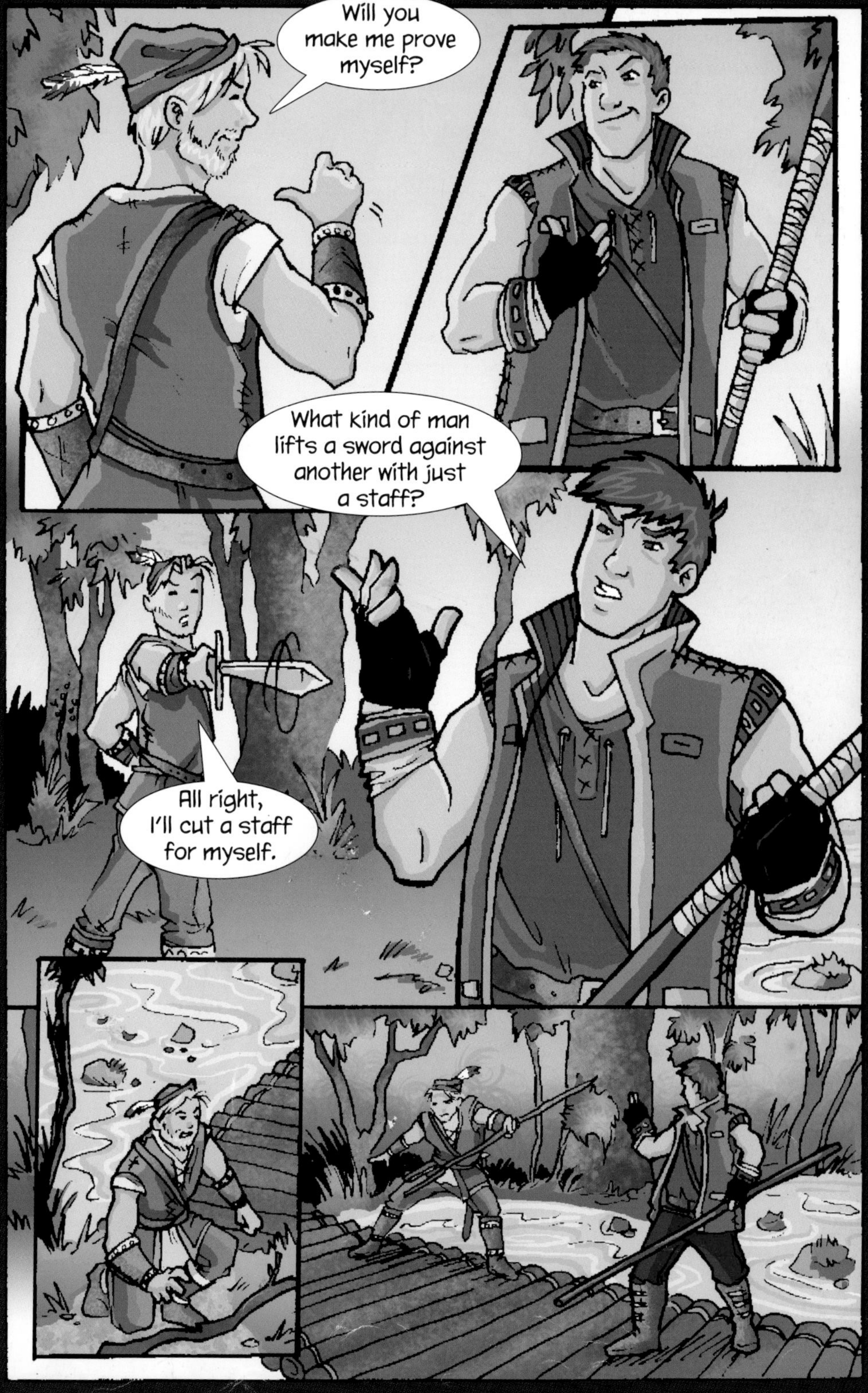
Will you make me prove myself?
What kind of man lifts a sword against another with just a staff?
All right, I'll cut a staff for myself.

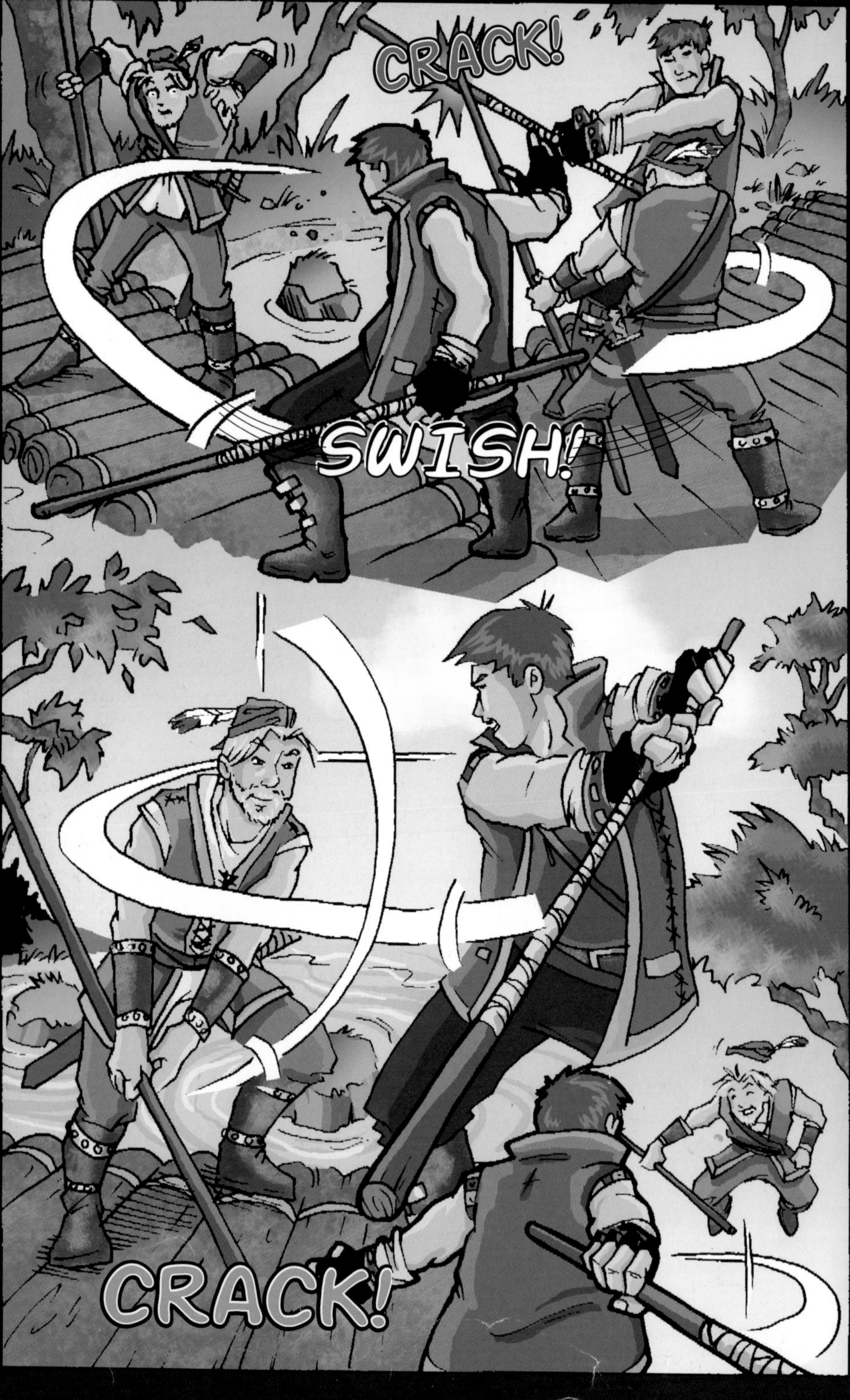
CRACK!
SWISH!
CRACK!

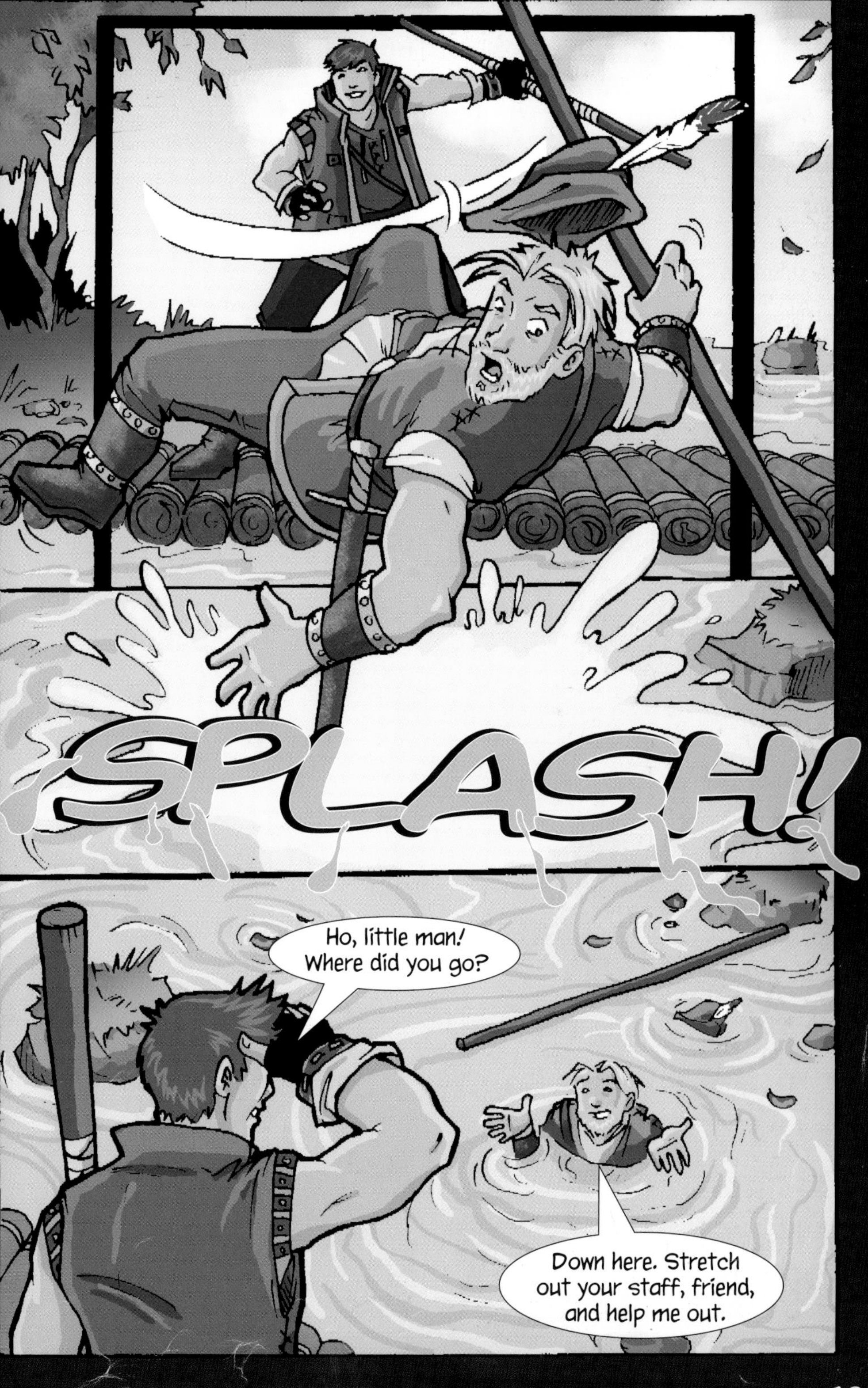
SPLASH!
Ho, little man! Where did you go?
Down here. Stretch out your staff, friend, and help me out.

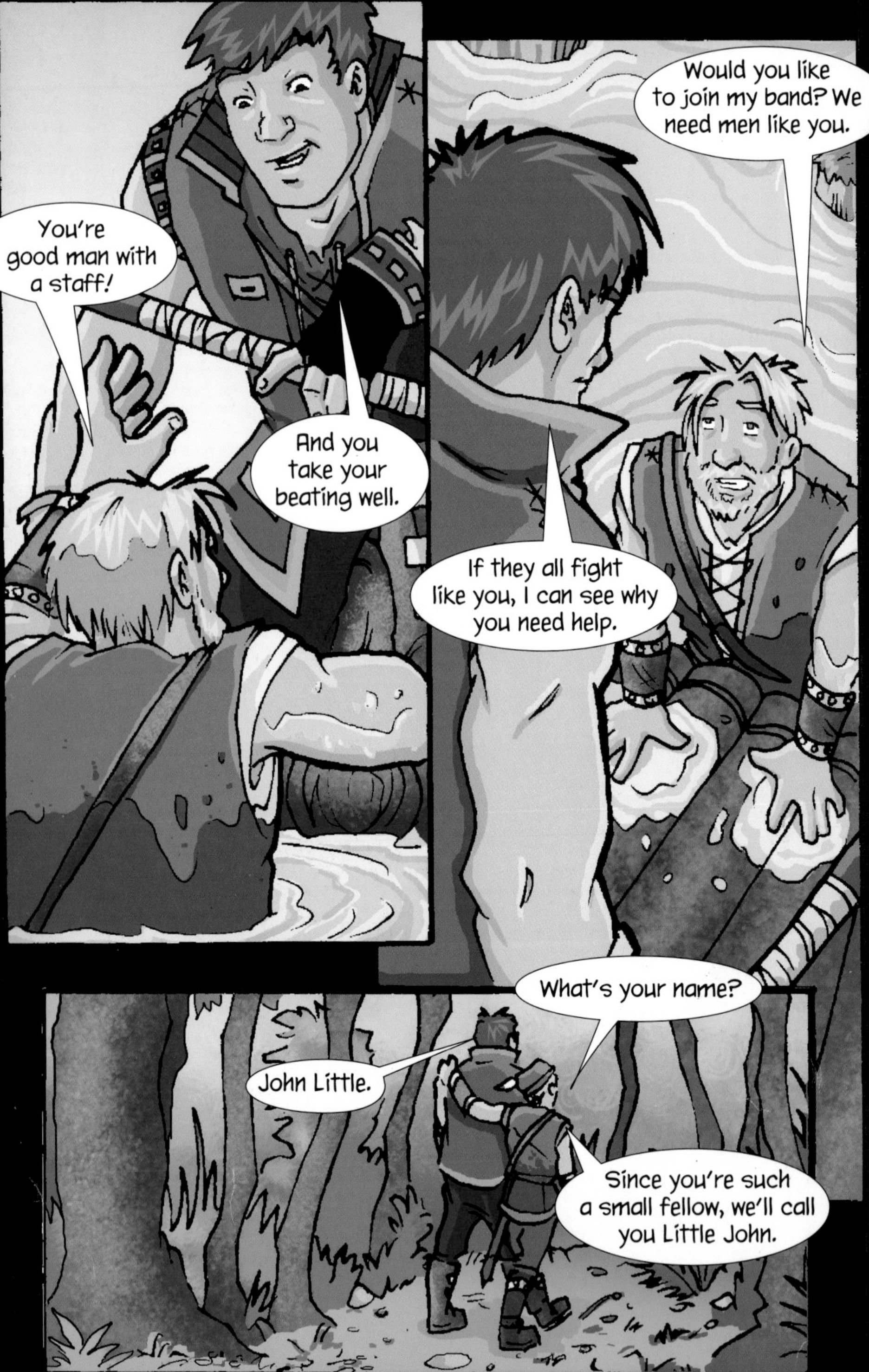
You're a good man with a staff!
And you take your beating well.
Would you like to join my band? We need men like you.
If they all fight like you, I can see why you need help.
What's your name?
John Little.
Since you're such a small fellow, we'll call you Little John.

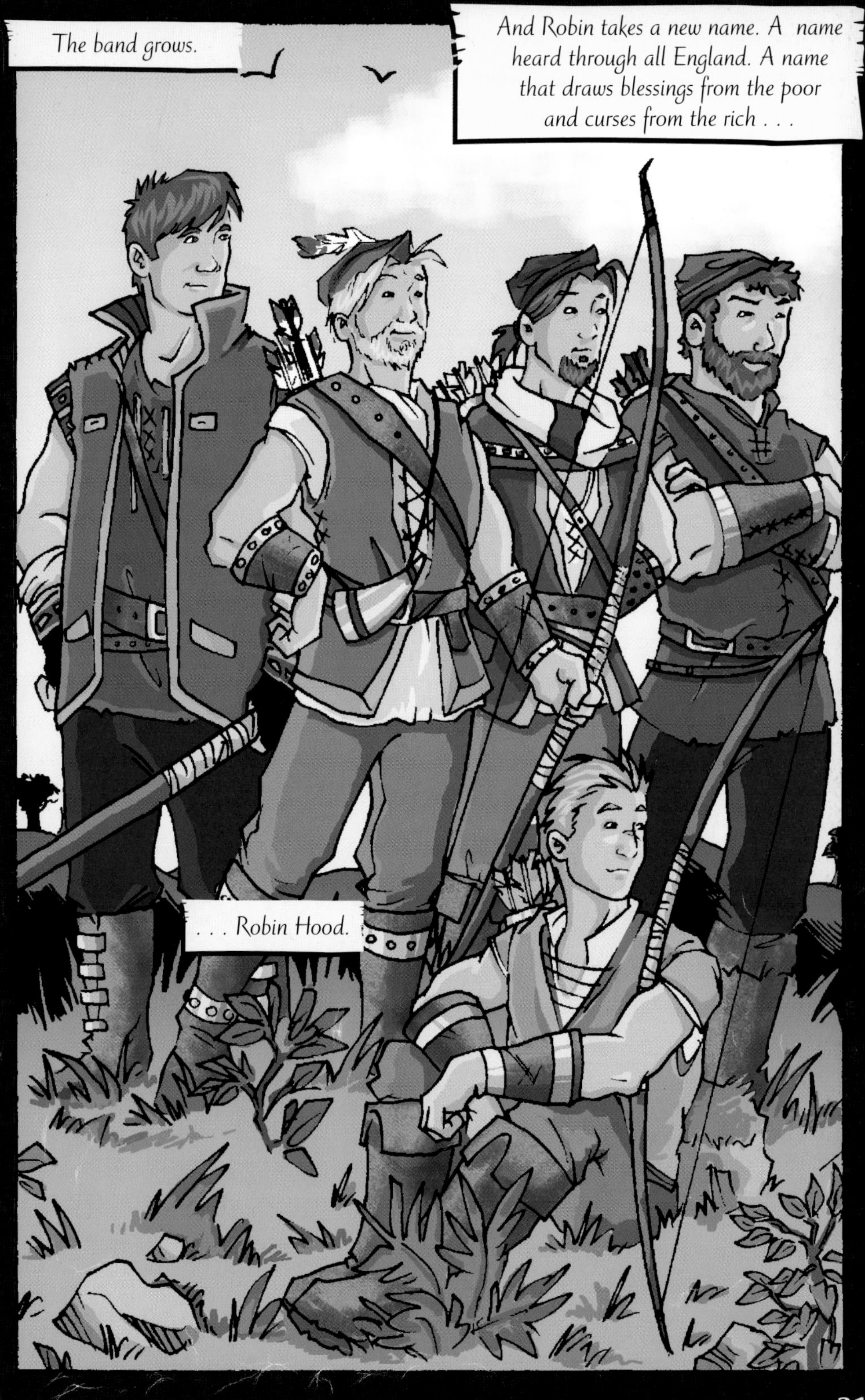
The band grows.
And Robin takes a new name. A name heard through all England. A name that draws blessings from the poor and curses from the rich . . .
. . . Robin Hood.

Chapter 2 -Robin the Match Maker

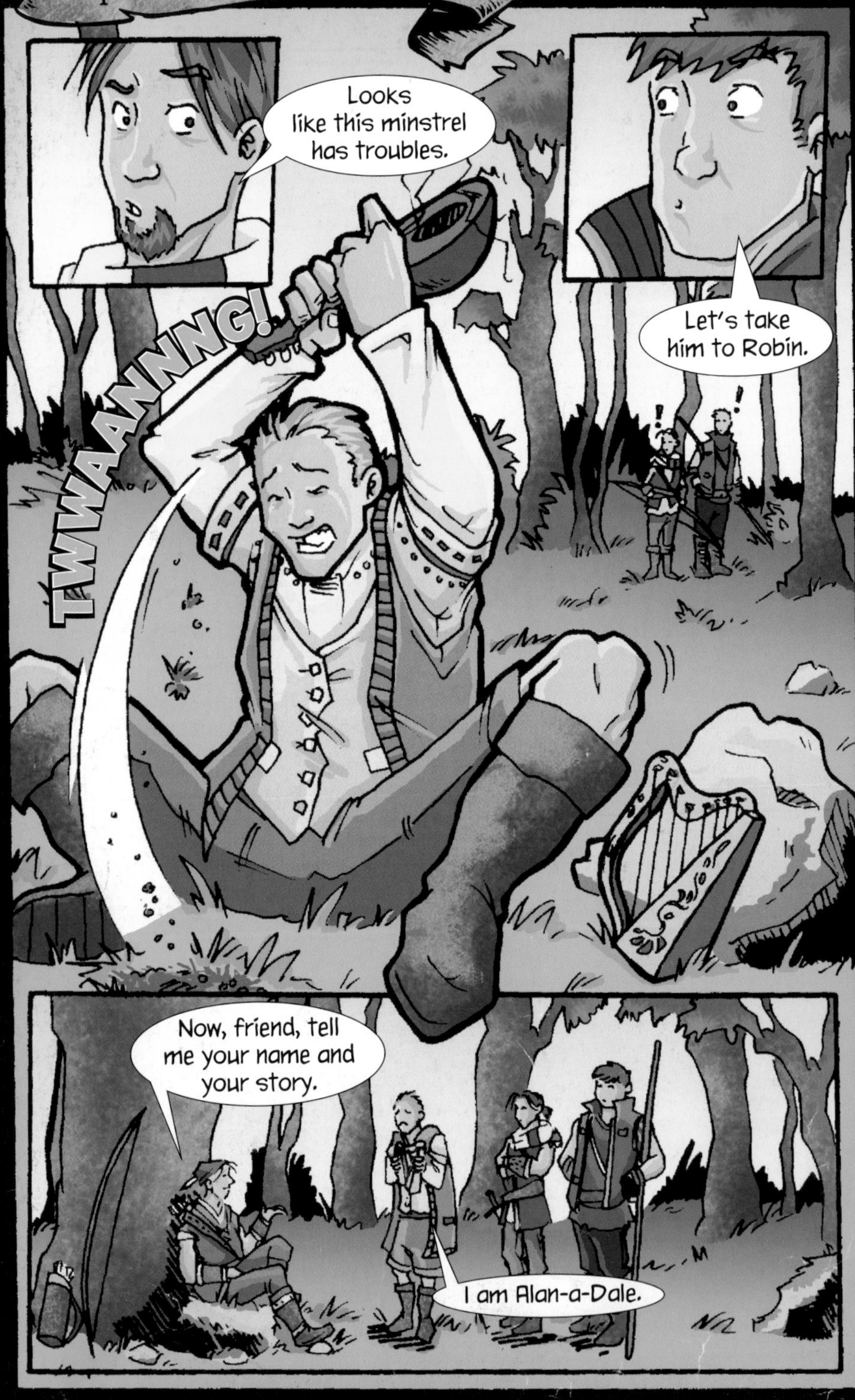

Looks like this minstrel has troubles.
Let's take him to Robin.
TWWAANNNG!
Now, friend, tell me your name and your story.
I am Alan-a-Dale.

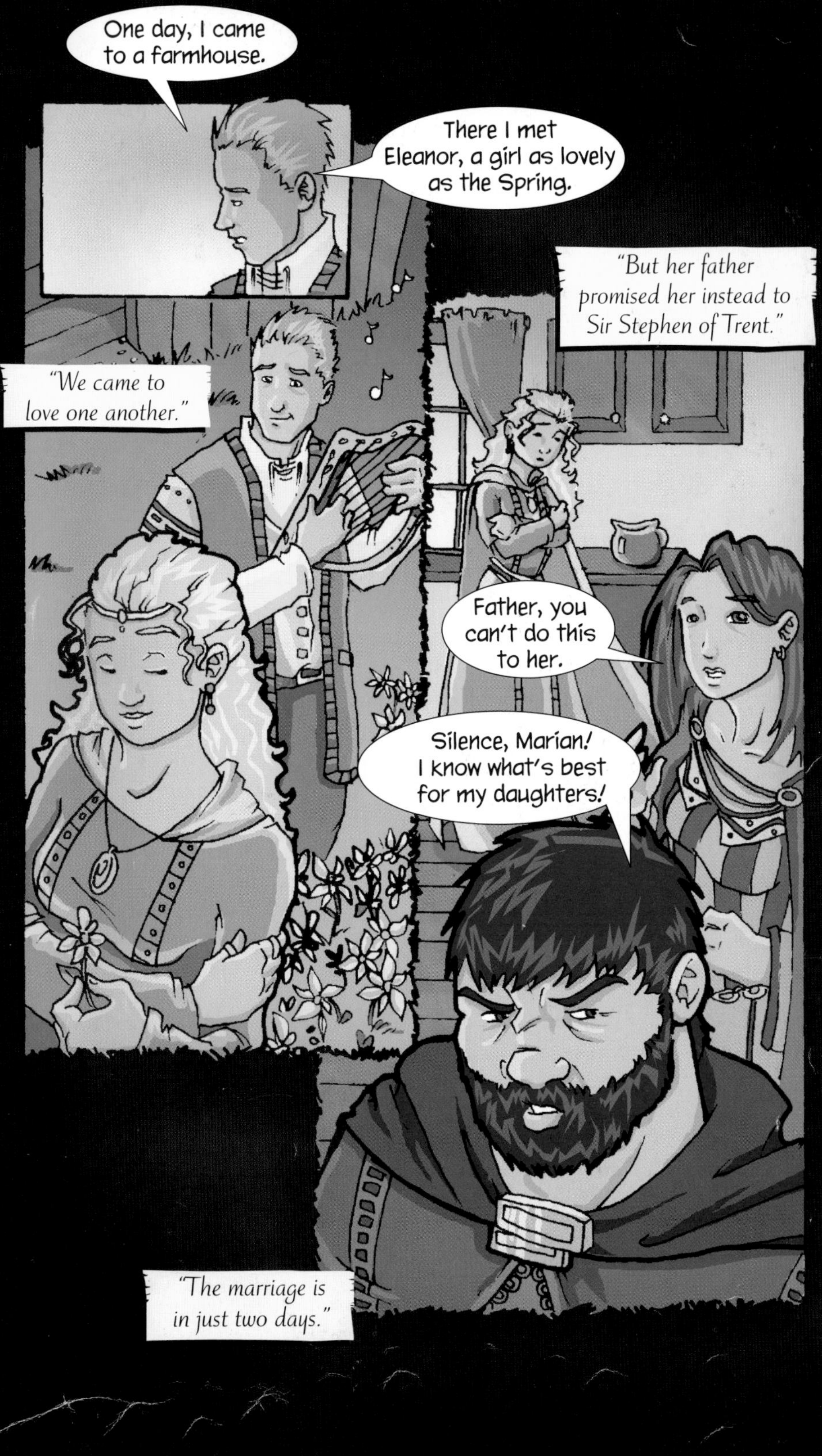
One day, I came to a farmhouse.
There I met Eleanor, a girl as lovely as the Spring.
"We came to love one another."
"But her father promised her instead to Sir Stephen of Trent."
Father, you can't do this to her.
Silence, Marian! I know what's best for my daughters!
"The marriage is in just two days."

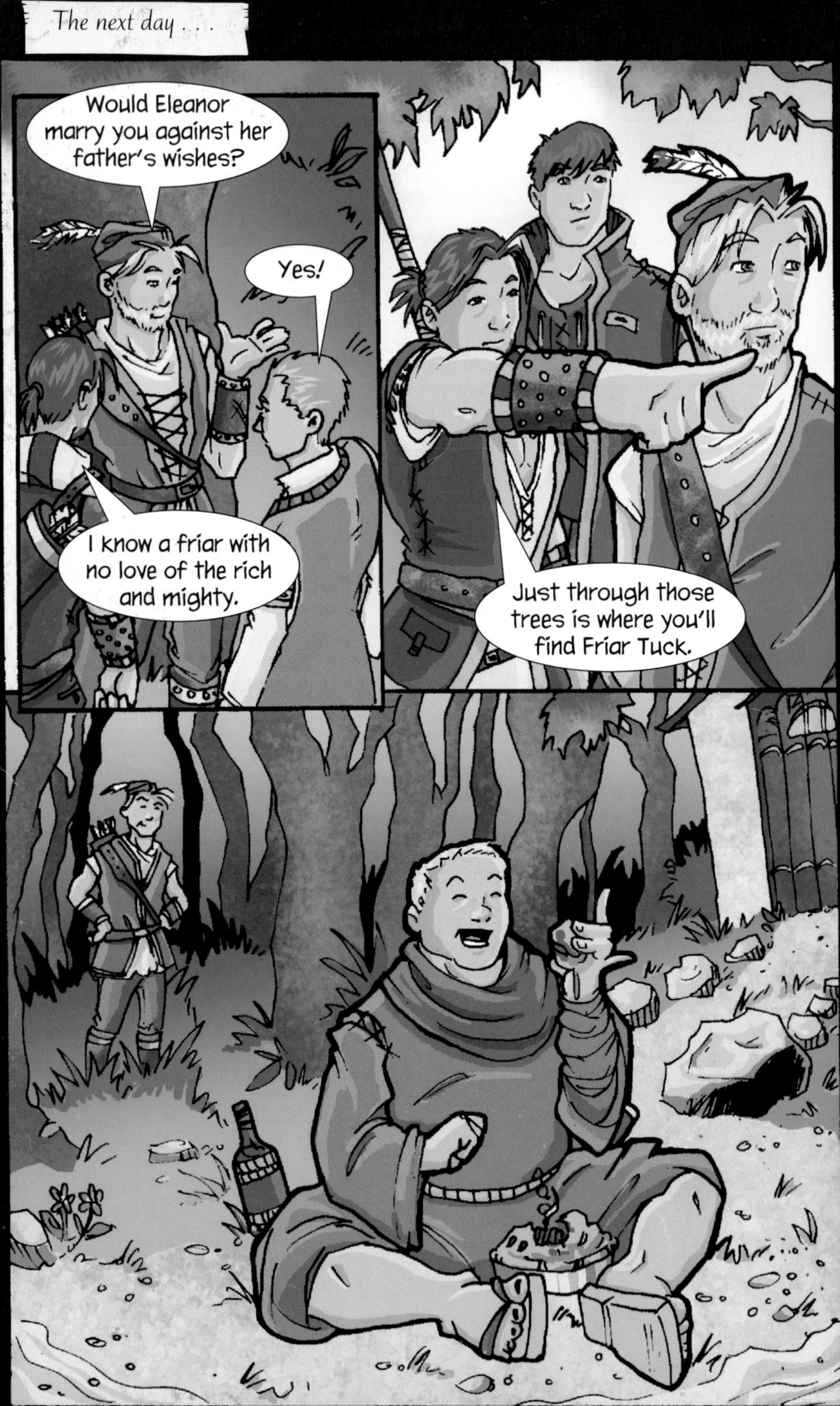
The next day . . .
Would Eleanor marry you against her father's wishes?
Yes!
I know a friar with no love of the rich and mighty.
Just through those trees is where you'll find Friar Tuck.

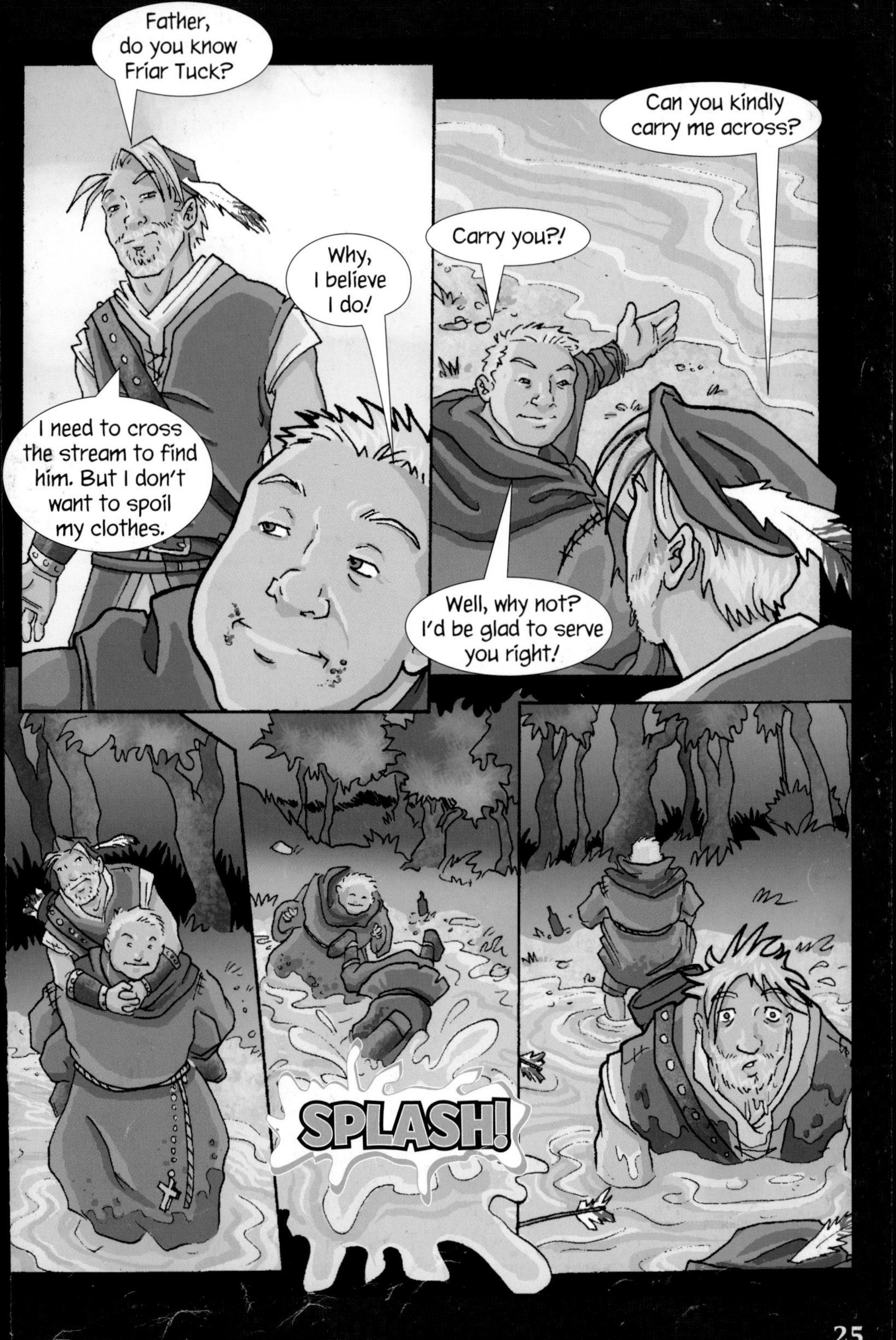

Father, do you know Friar Tuck?
I need to cross the stream to find him. But I don't want to spoil my clothes.
Why, I believe I do!
Can you kindly carry me across?
Carry you?!
Well, why not? I'd be glad to serve you right!
SPLASH!

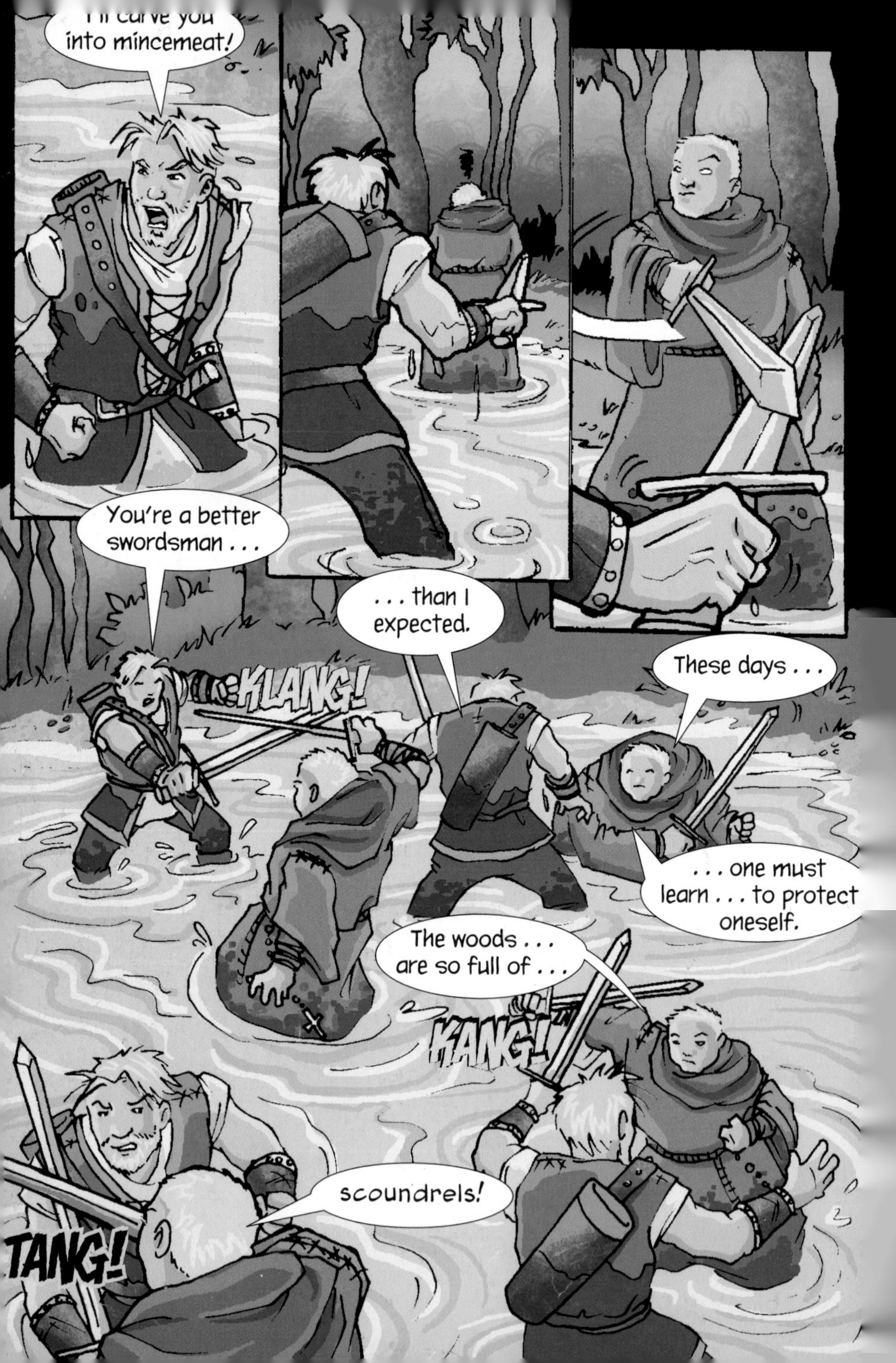
I'll carve you into mincemeat!
You're a better swordsman . . .
. . . than I expected.
KLANG!
These days . . .
. . . one must learn . . . to protect oneself.
The woods . . . are so full of . . .
KANG!
scoundrels!
TANG!

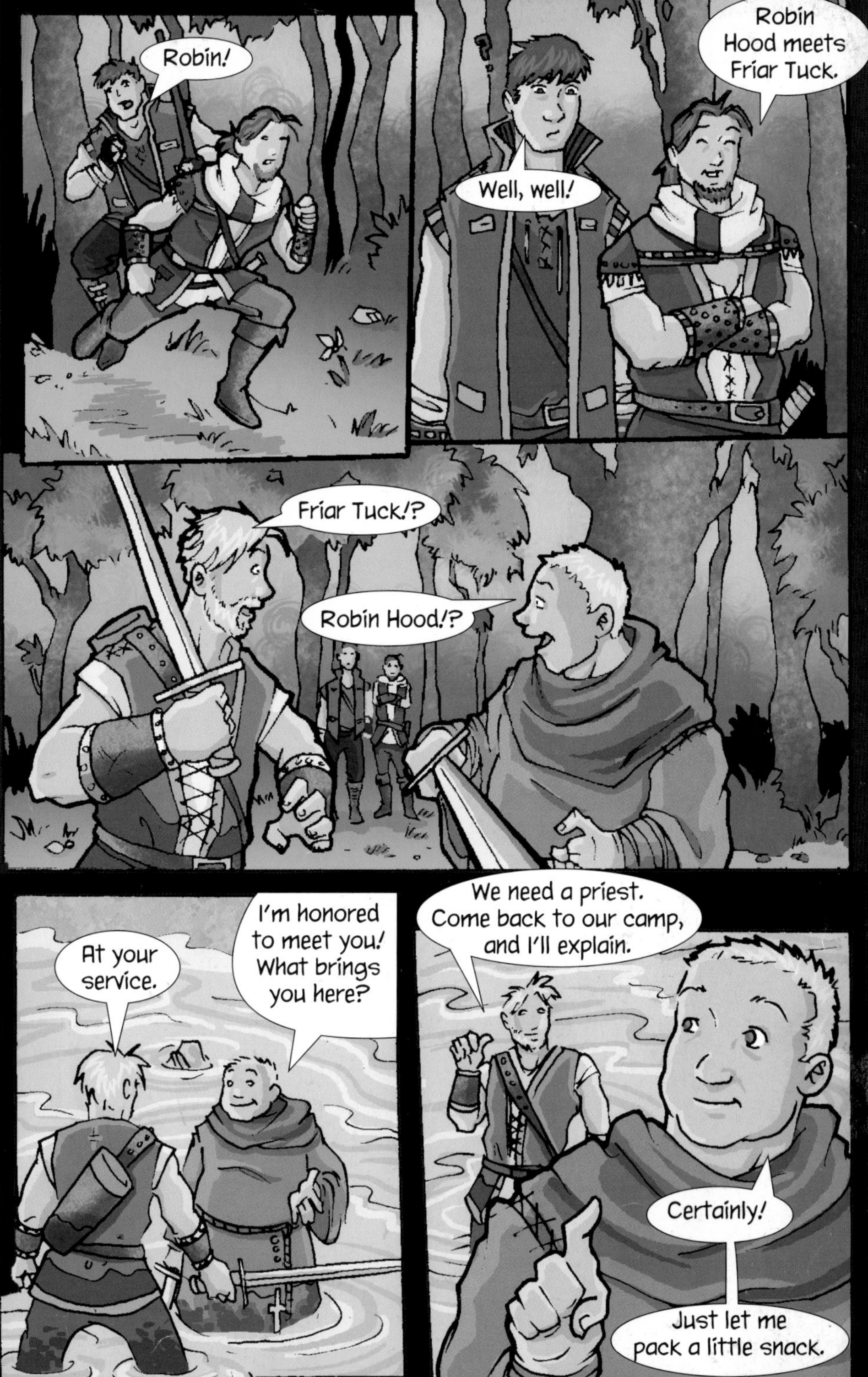
Robin!
Robin Hood meets Friar Tuck.
Well, well!
Friar Tuck!?
Robin Hood!?
At your service.
I'm honored to meet you! What brings you here?
We need a priest. Come back to our camp, and I'll explain.
Certainly!
Just let me pack a little snack.

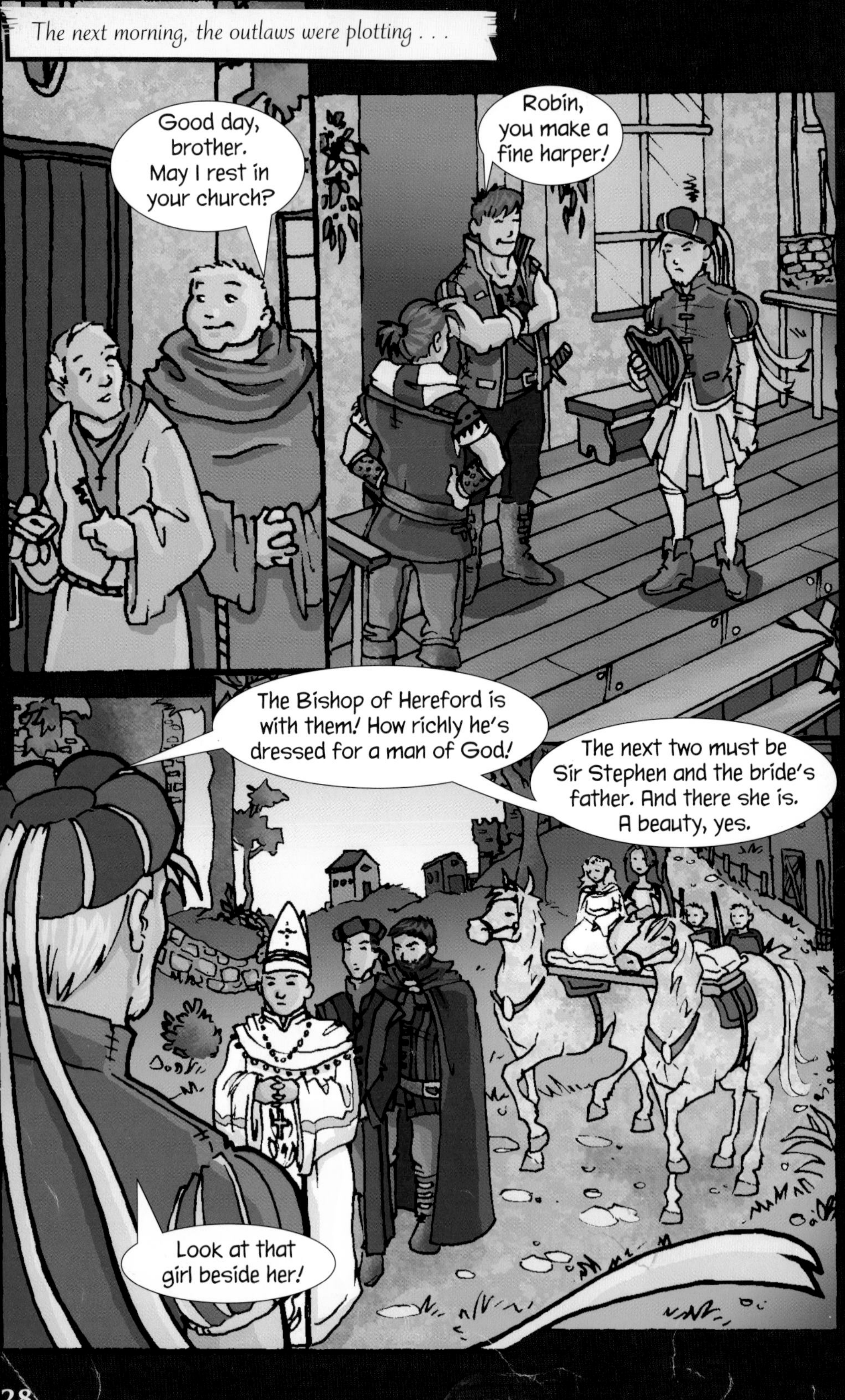
The next morning, the outlaws were plotting . . .
Good day, brother. May I rest in your church?
Robin, you make a fine harper!
The Bishop of Hereford is with them! How richly he's dressed for a man of God!
The next two must be Sir Stephen and the bride's father. And there she is. A beauty, yes.
Look at that girl beside her!

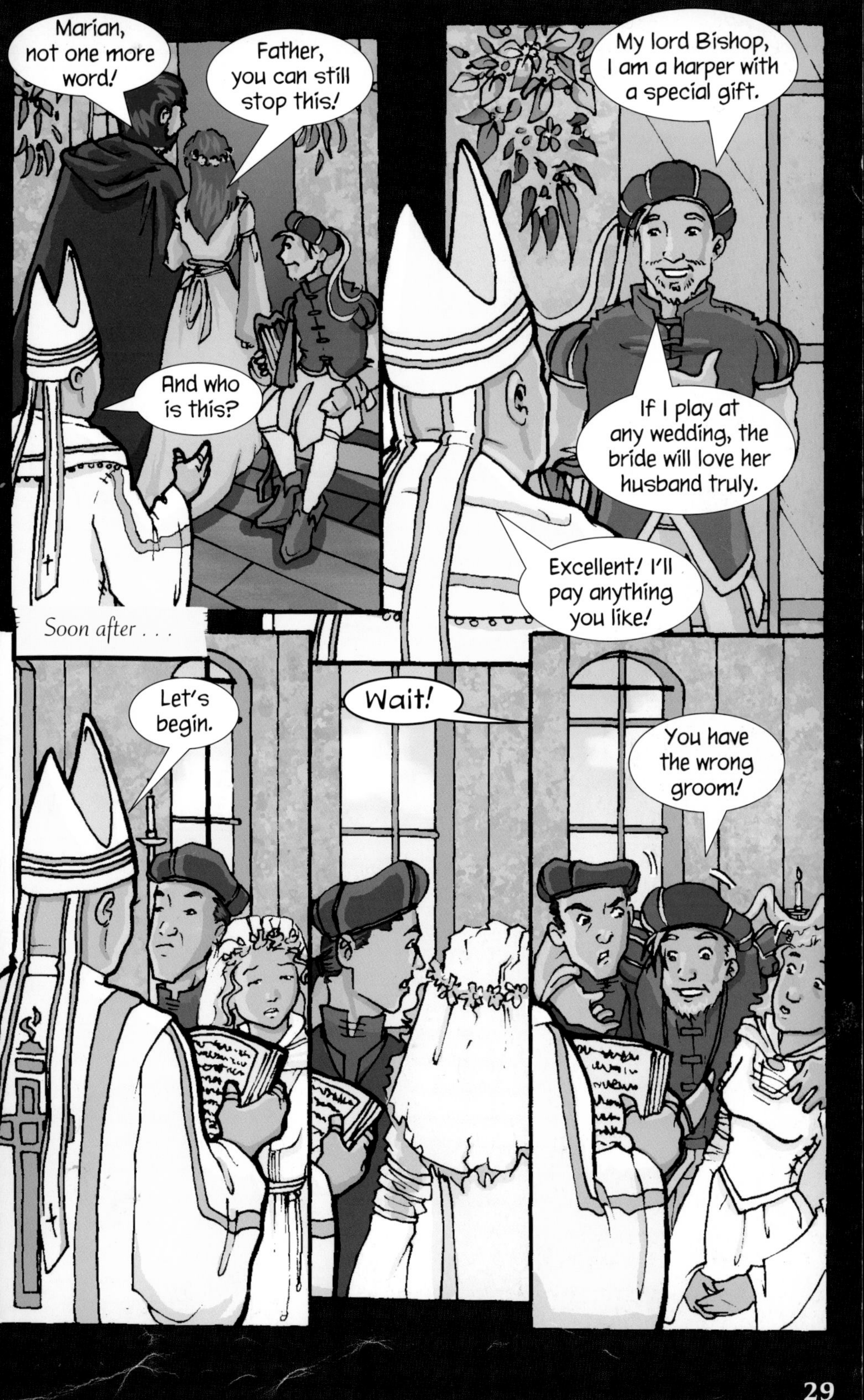
Marian, not one more word!
Father, you can still stop this!
And who is this?
My lord Bishop, I am a harper with a special gift.
If I play at any wedding, the bride will love her husband truly.
Excellent! I'll pay anything you like!
Soon after . . .
Let's begin.
Wait!
You have the wrong groom!

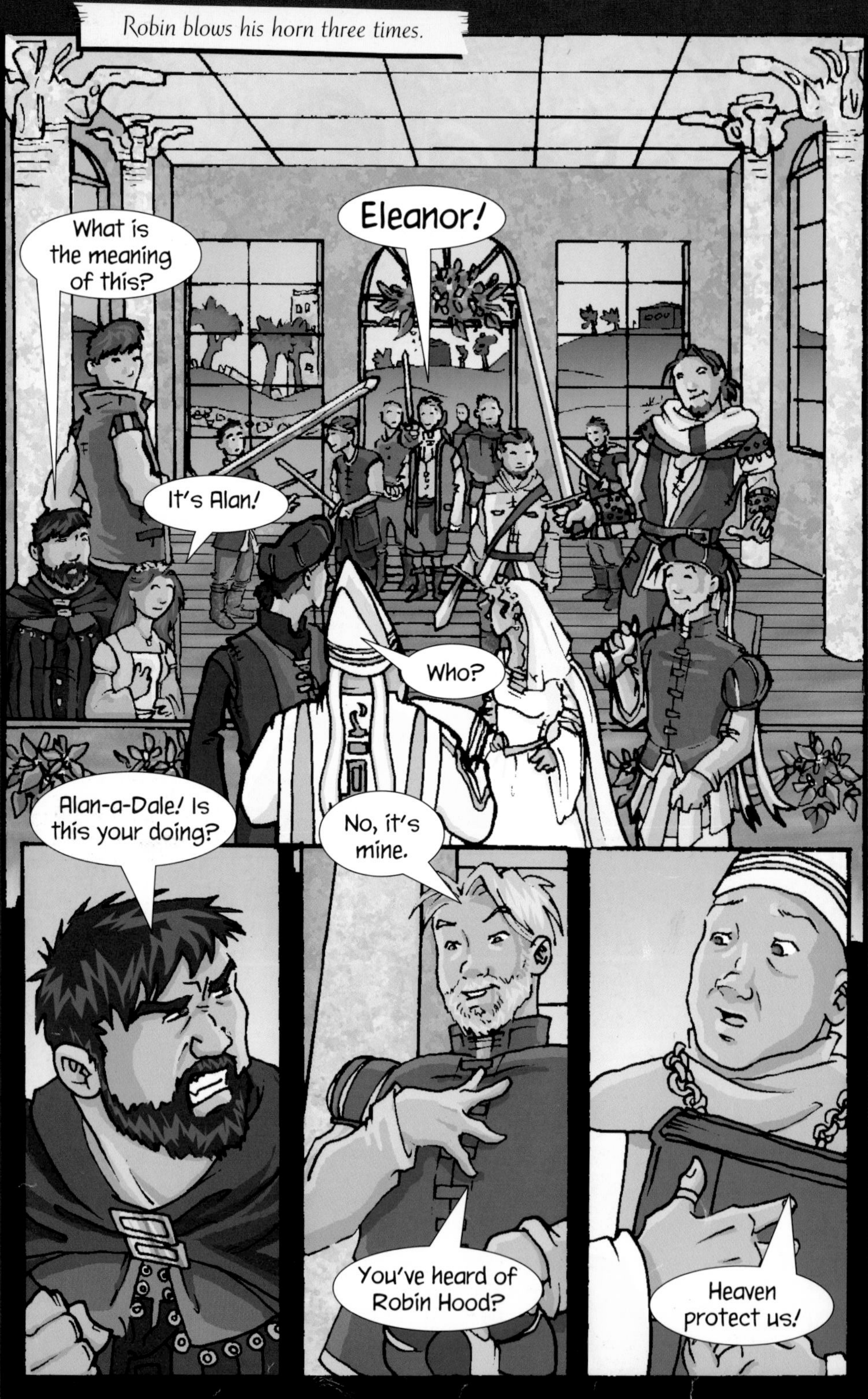
Robin blows his horn three times.
What is the meaning of this?
Eleanor!
It's Alan!
Who?
Alan-a-Dale! Is this your doing?
No, it's mine.
You've heard of Robin Hood?
Heaven protect us!

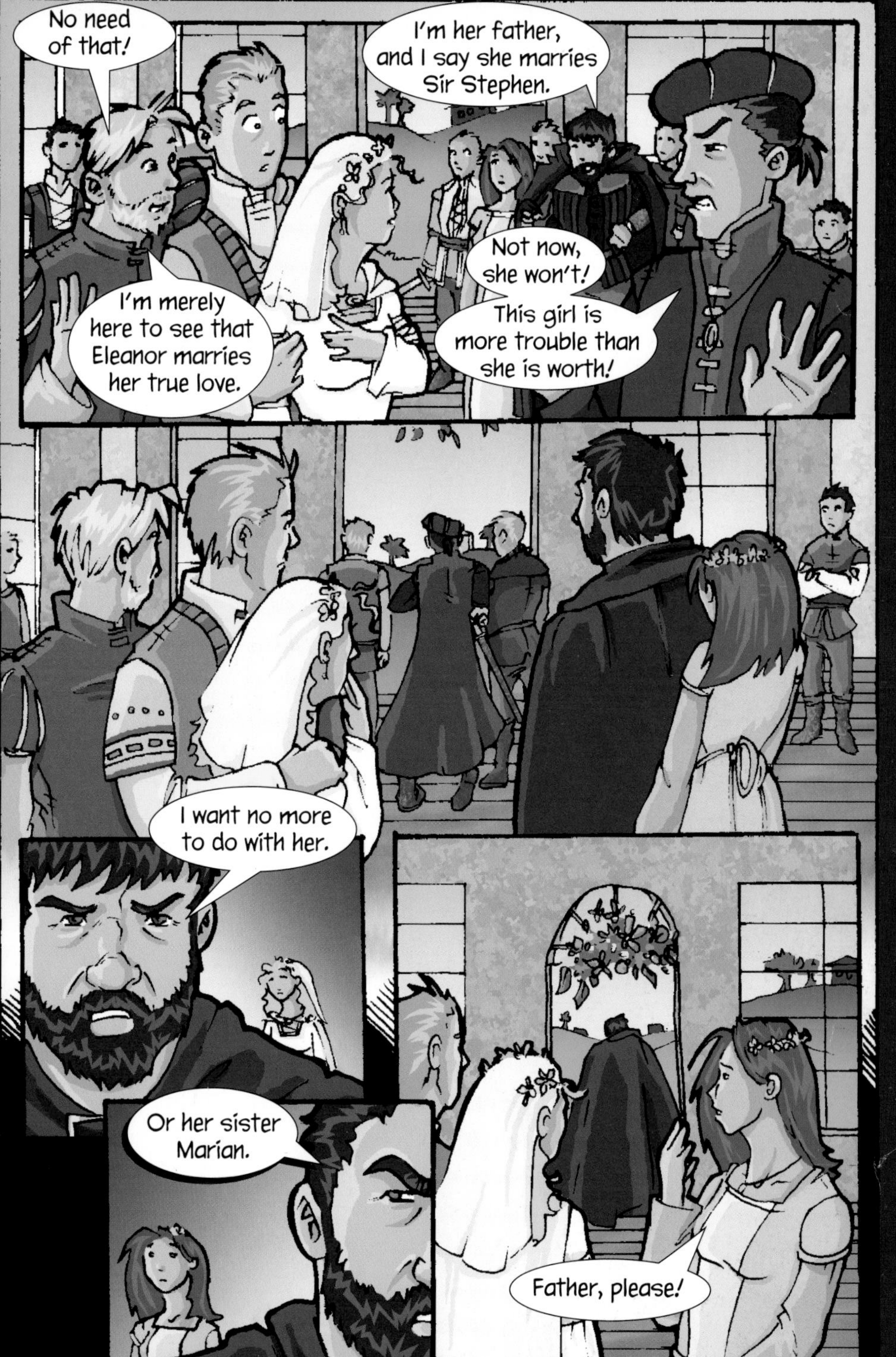
No need of that!
I'm her father, and I say she marries Sir Stephen.
I'm merely here to see that Eleanor marries her true love.
Not now, she won't!
This girl is more trouble than she is worth!
I want no more to do with her.
Or her sister Marian.
Father, please!

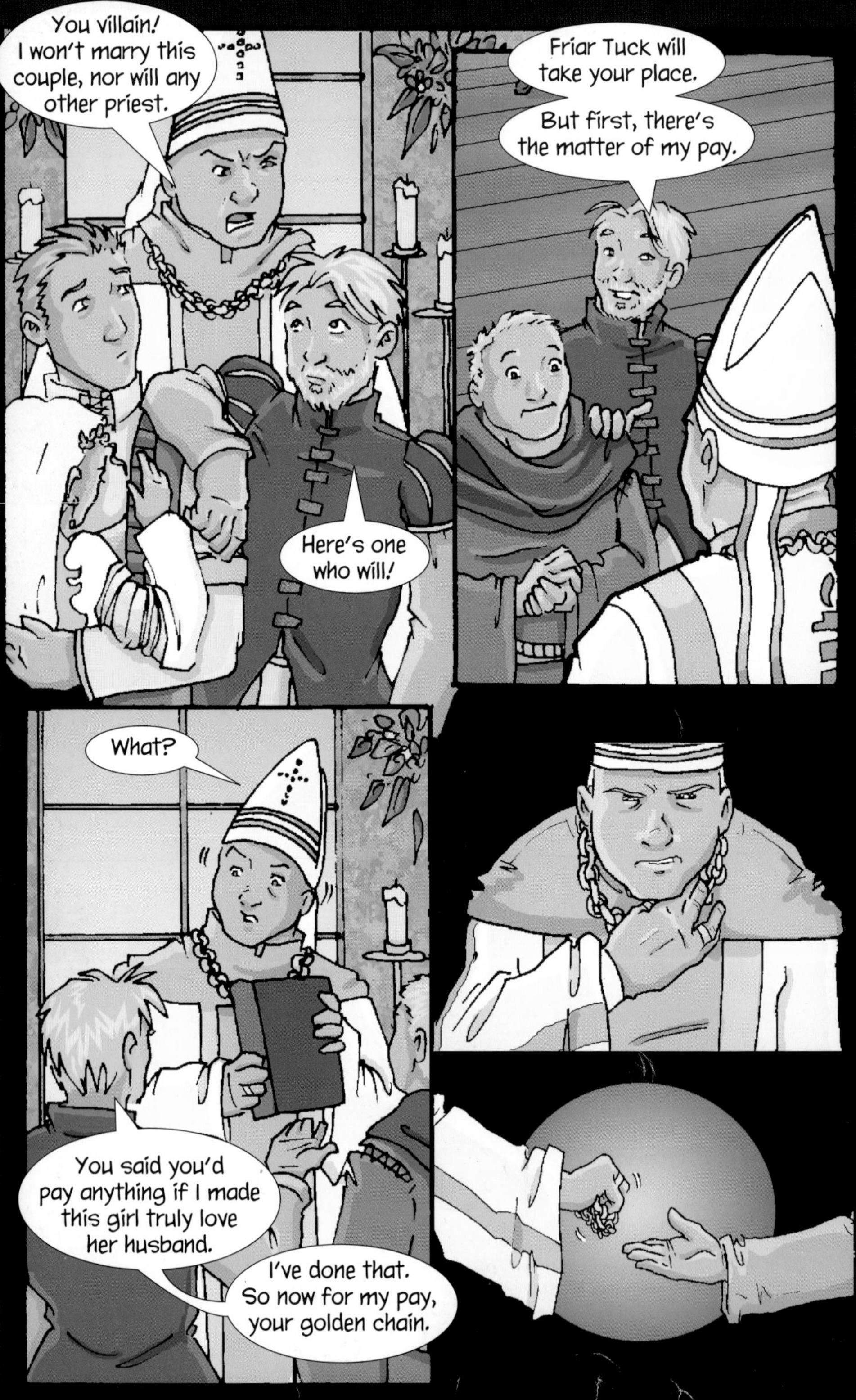
You villain! I won't marry this couple, nor will any other priest.
Here's one who will!
Friar Tuck will take your place.
But first, there's the matter of my pay.
What?
You said you'd pay anything if I made this girl truly love her husband.
I've done that. So now for my pay, your golden chain.

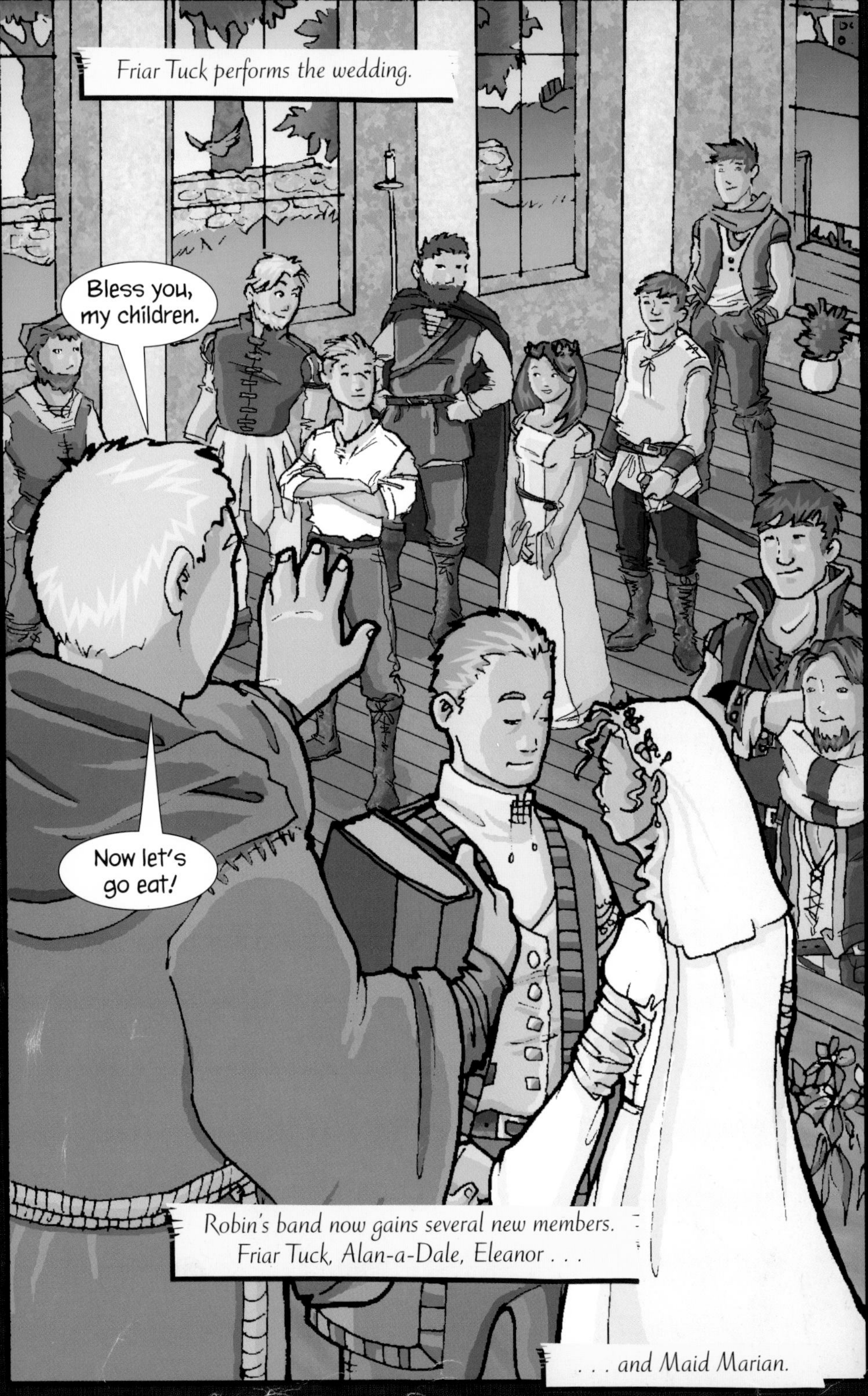

Friar Tuck performs the wedding.
Bless you, my children.
Now let's go eat!
Robin's band now gains several new members. Friar Tuck, Alan-a-Dale, Eleanor . . .
. . . and Maid Marian.

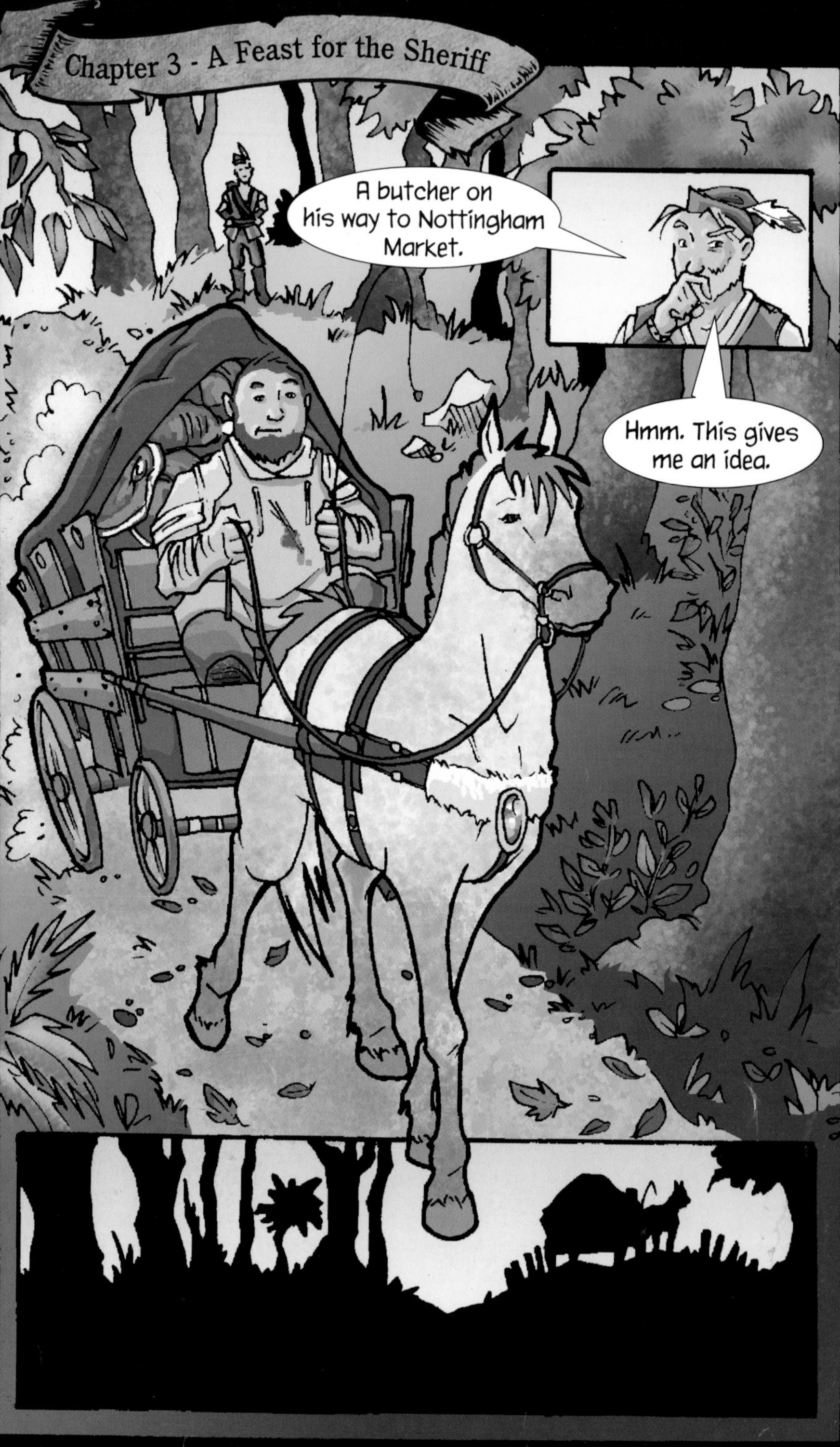
Chapter 3 - A Feast for the Sheriff
A butcher on his way to Nottingham Market.
Hmm. This gives me an idea.

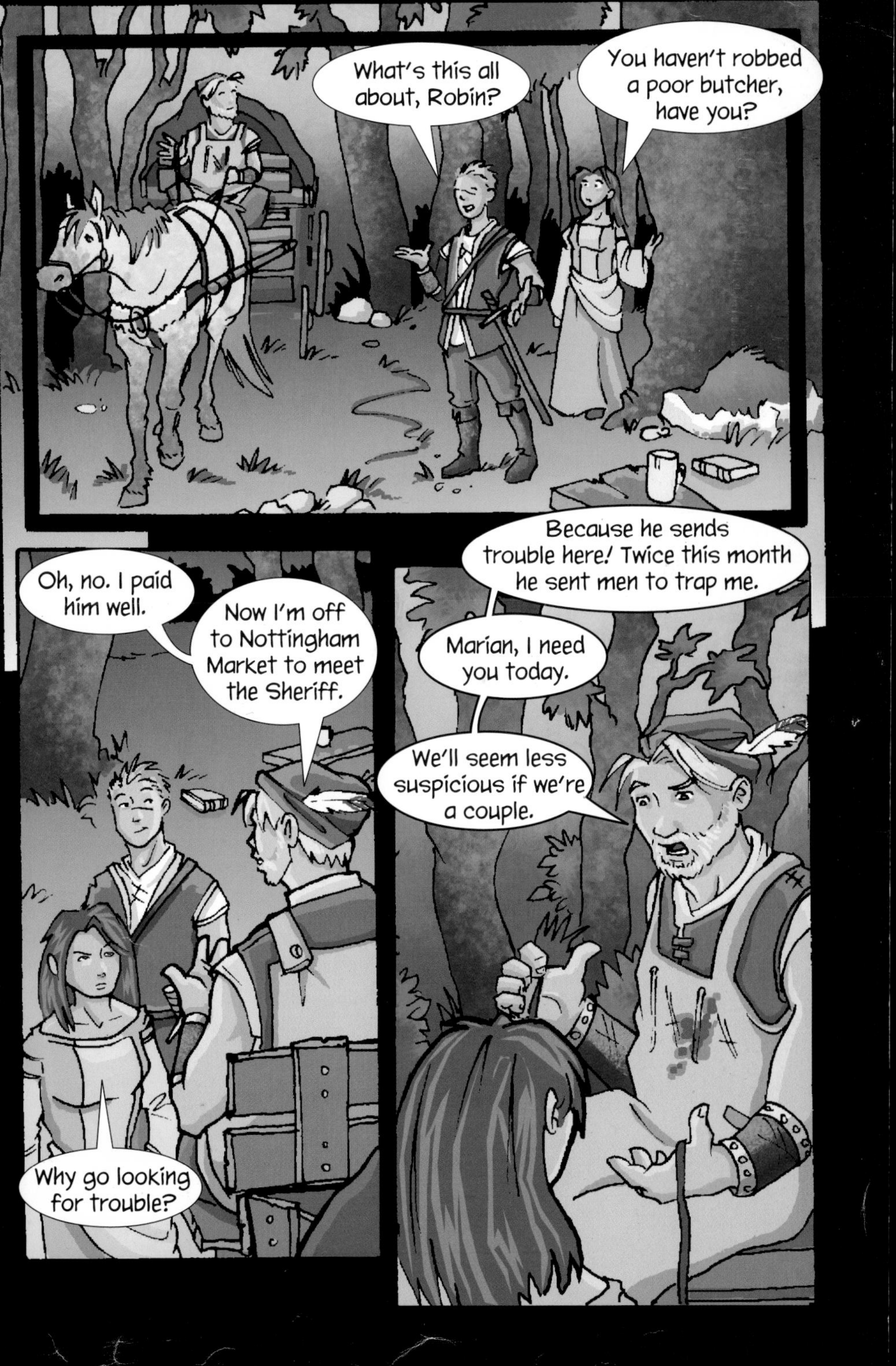
What's this all about, Robin?
You haven't robbed a poor butcher, have you?
Oh, no. I paid him well.
Now I'm off to Nottingham Market to meet the Sheriff.
Why go looking for trouble?
Because he sends trouble here! Twice this month he sent men to trap me.
Marian, I need you today.
We'll seem less suspicious if we're a couple.

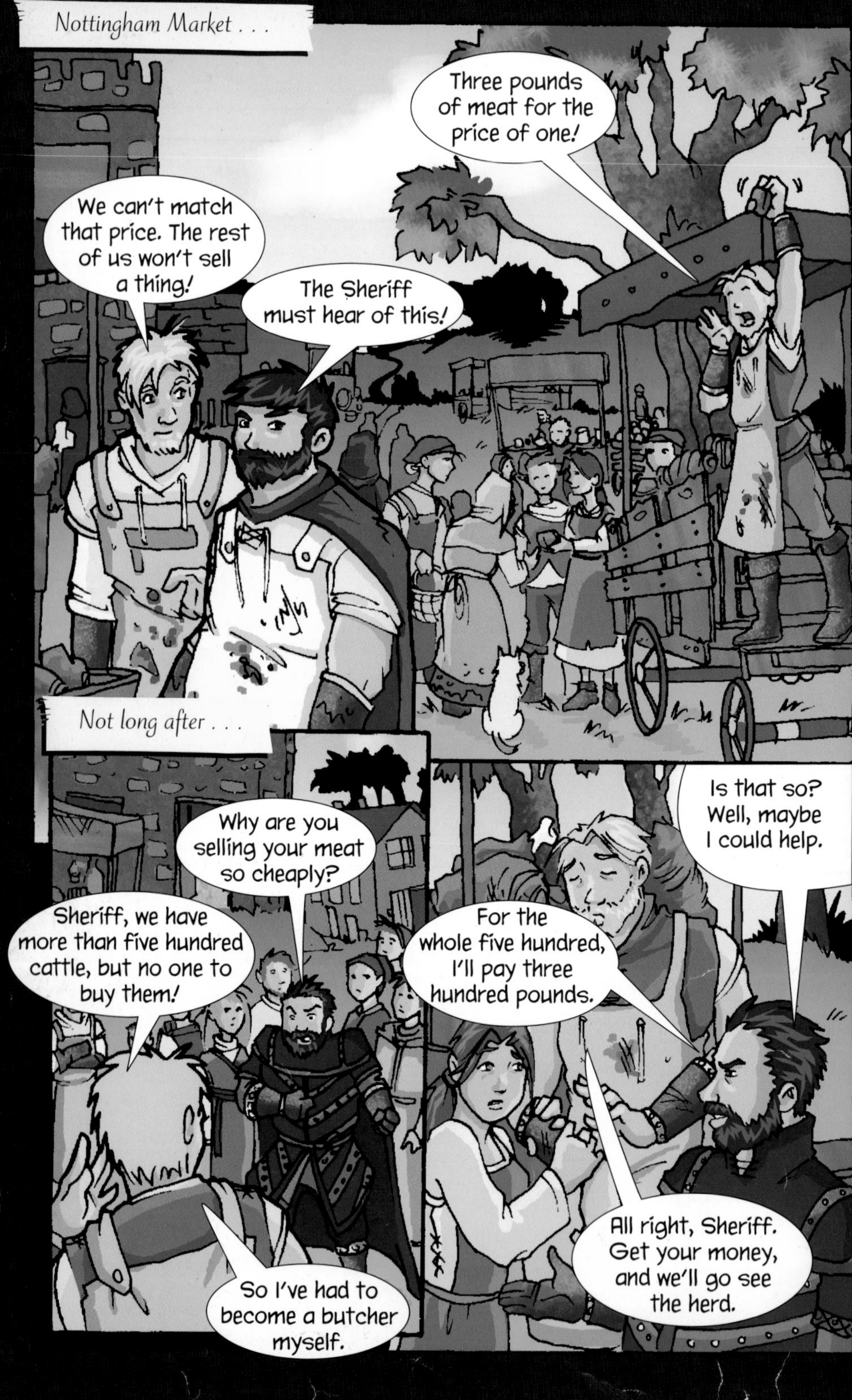
Nottingham Market . . .
Three pounds of meat for the price of one!
We can't match that price. The rest of us won't sell a thing!
The Sheriff must hear of this!
Not long after . . .
Why are you selling your meat so cheaply?
Sheriff, we have more than five hundred cattle, but no one to buy them!
So I've had to become a butcher myself.
Is that so? Well, maybe I could help.
For the whole five hundred, I'll pay three hundred pounds.
All right, Sheriff. Get your money, and we'll go see the herd.

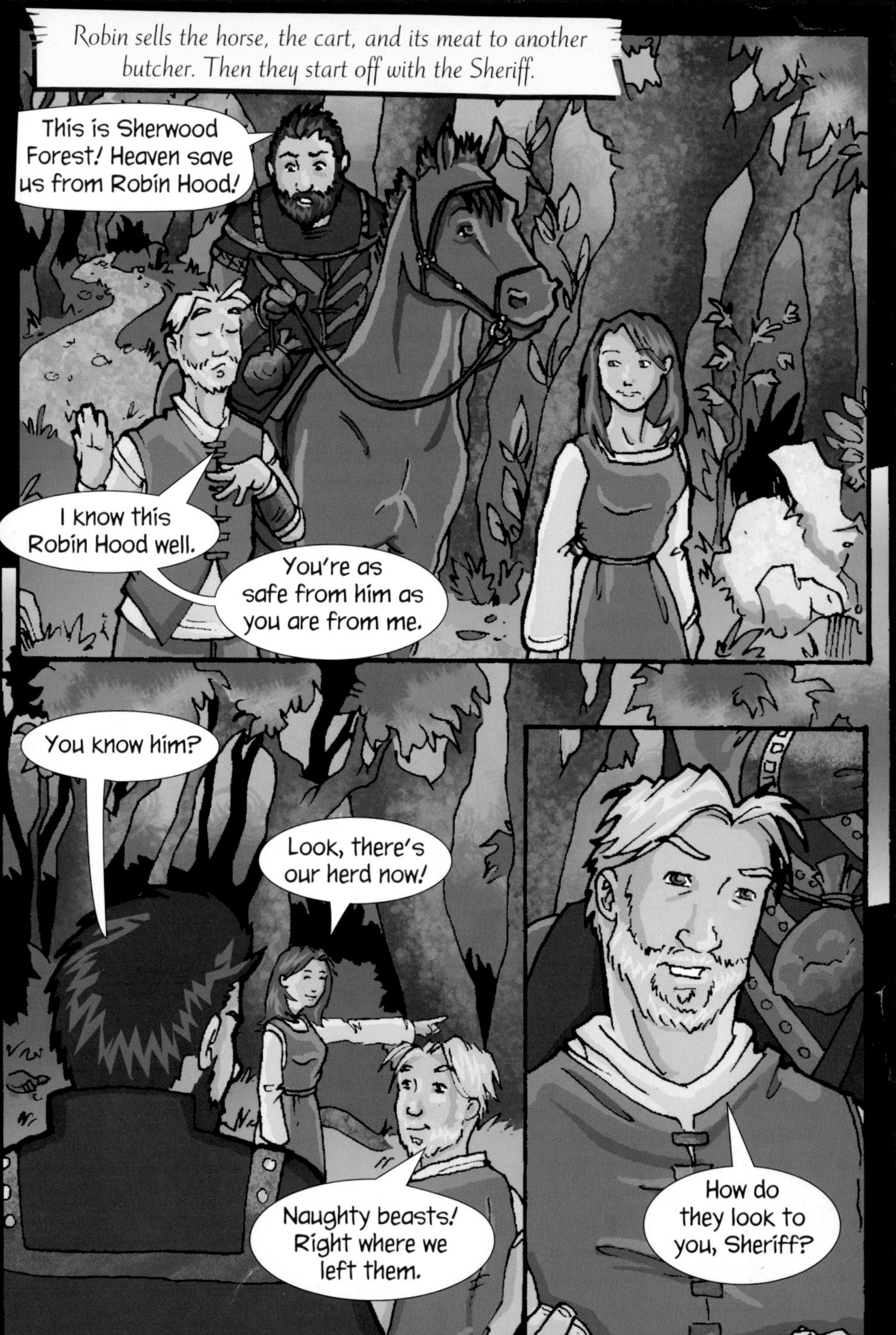
Robin sells the horse, the cart, and its meat to another butcher. Then they start off with the Sheriff.
This is Sherwood Forest! Heaven save us from Robin Hood!
I know this Robin Hood well.
You're as safe from him as you are from me.
You know him?
Look, there's our herd now!
Naughty beasts! Right where we left them.
How do they look to you, Sheriff?

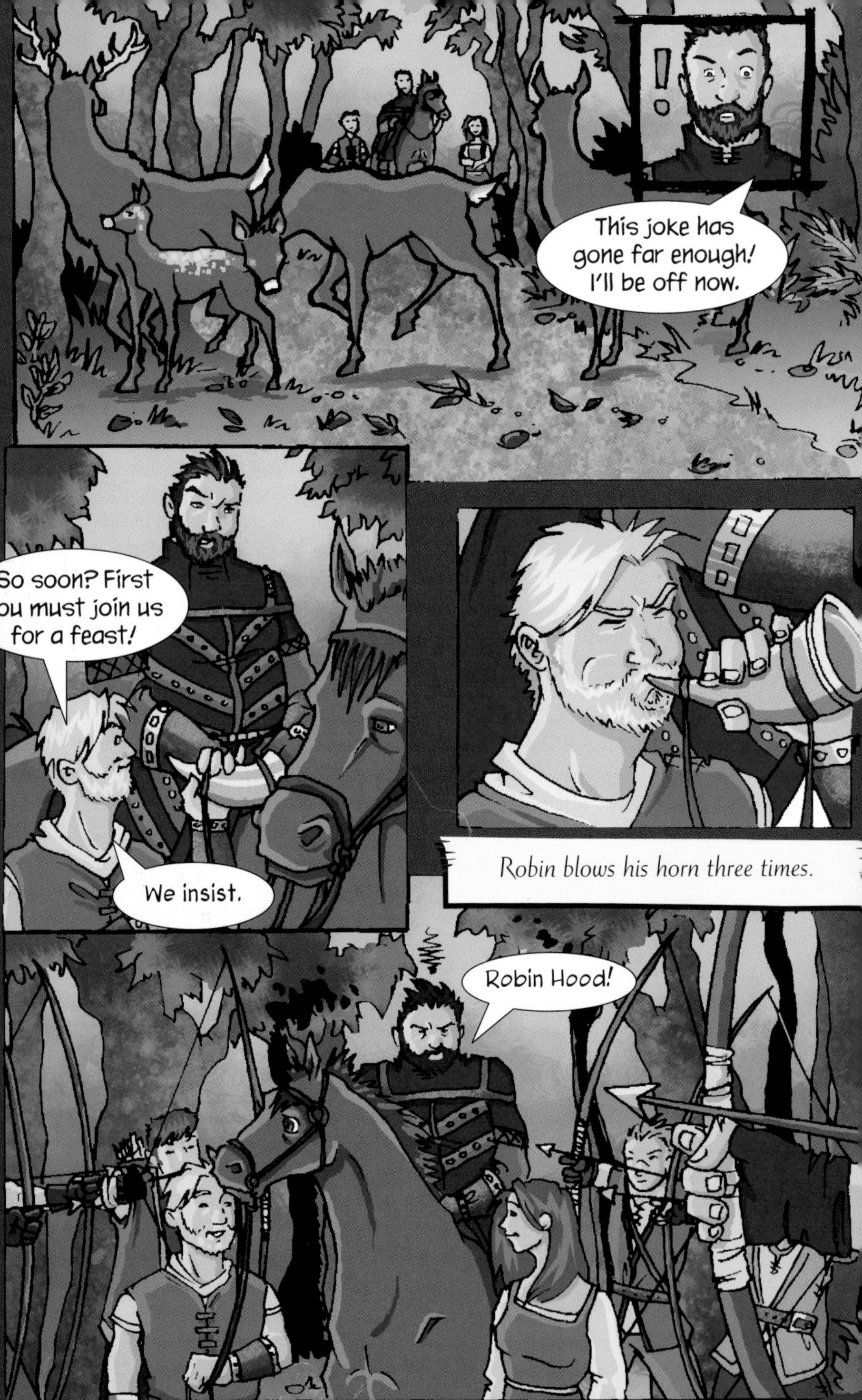
This joke has gone far enough! I'll be off now.
So soon? First you must join us for a feast!
We insist.
Robin blows his horn three times.
Robin Hood!

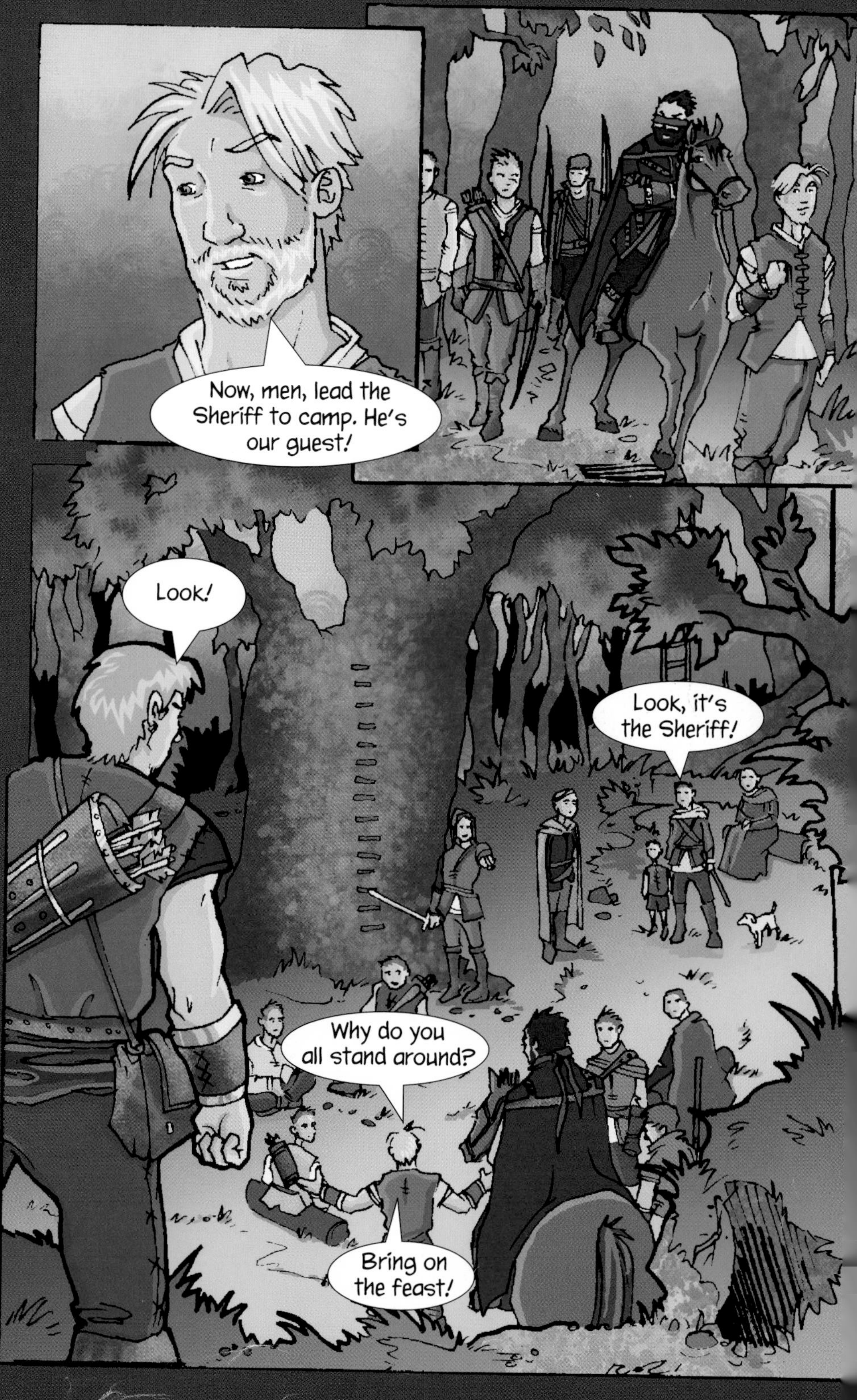
Now, men, lead the Sheriff to camp. He's our guest!
Look!
Look, it's the Sheriff!
Why do you all stand around?
Bring on the feast!

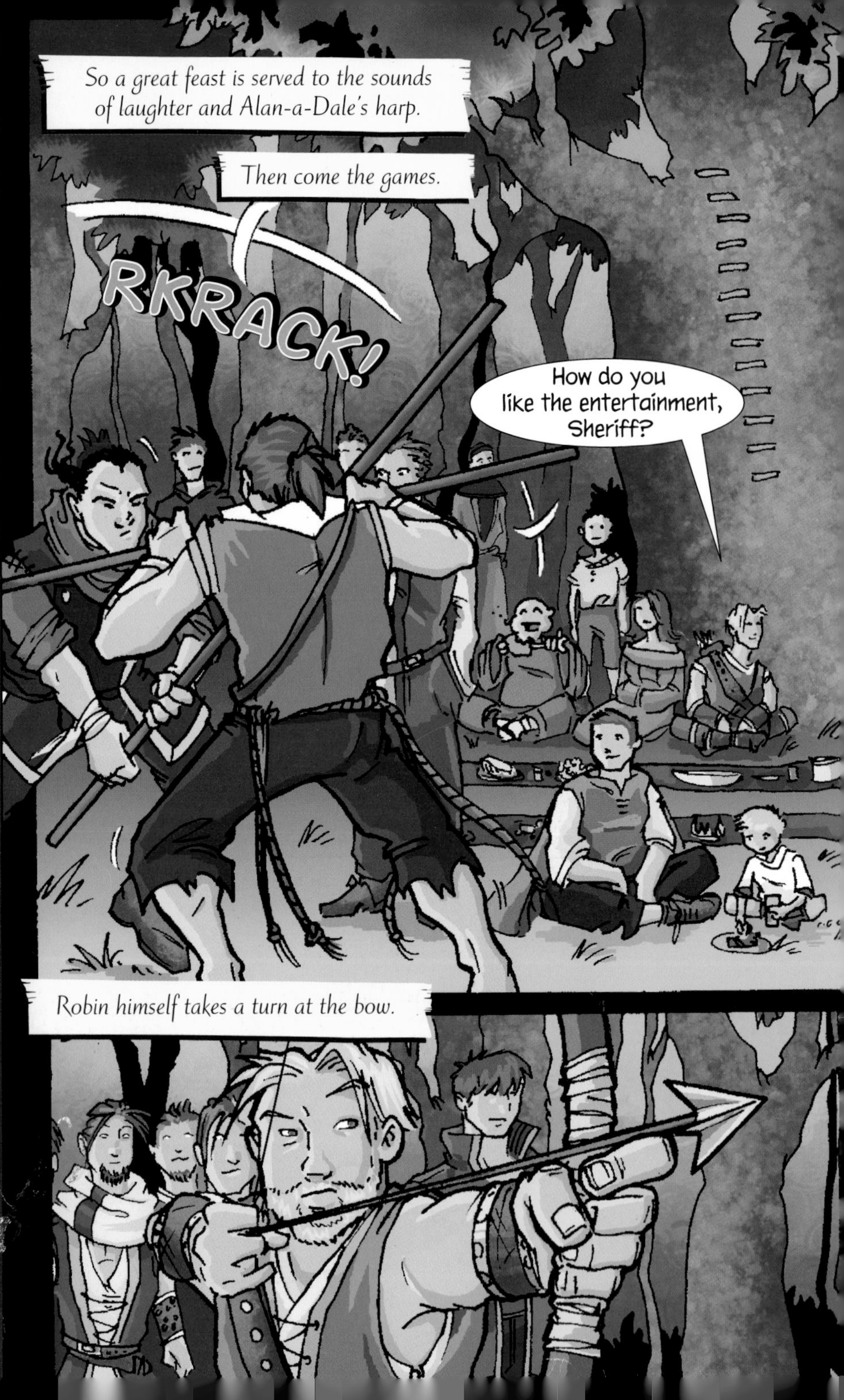
So a great feast is served to the sounds of laughter and Alan-a-Dale's harp.
Then come the games.
RKRACK!
How do you like the entertainment, Sheriff?
Robin himself takes a turn at the bow.

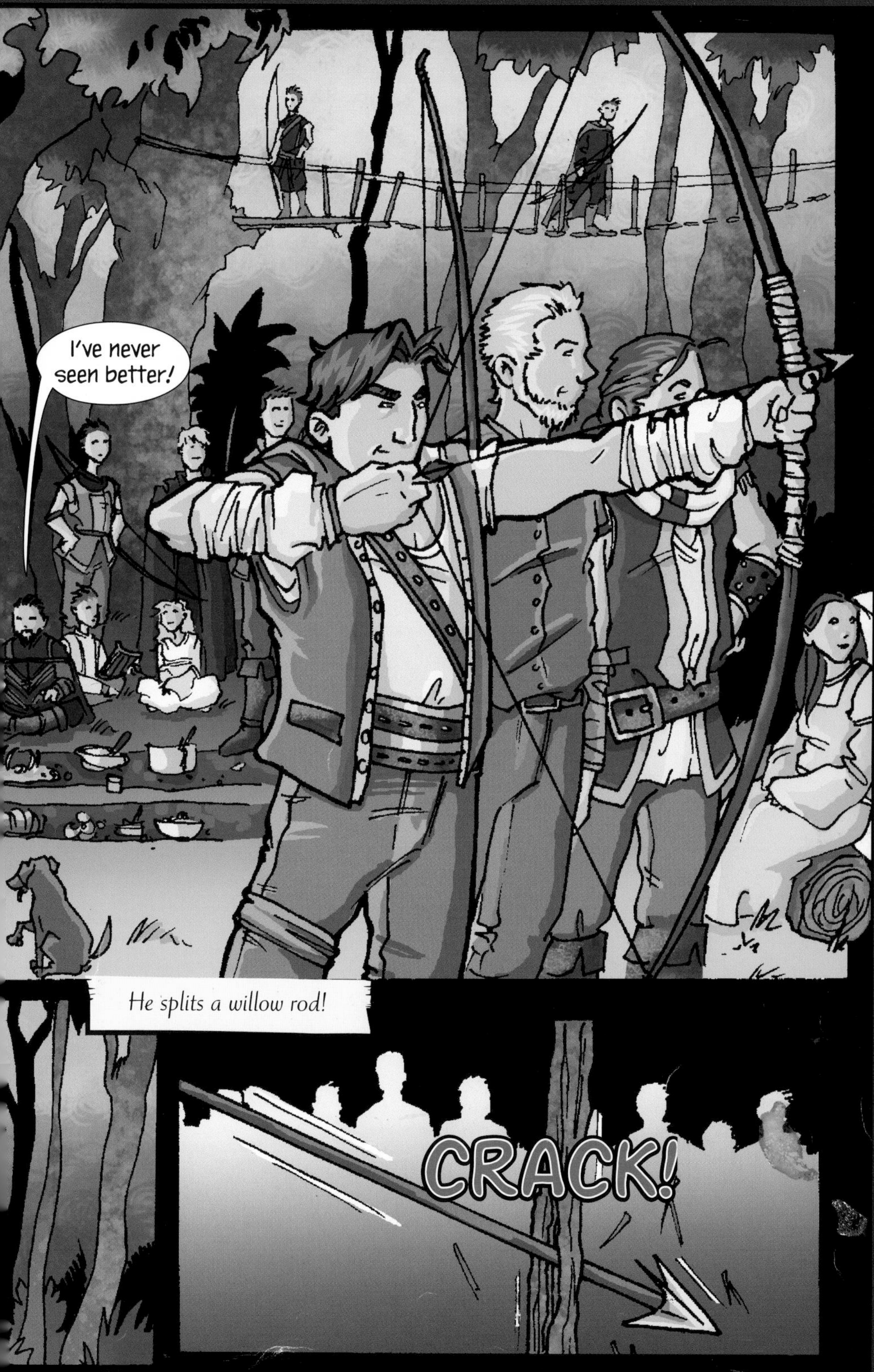
I've never seen better!
He splits a willow rod!
CRACK!

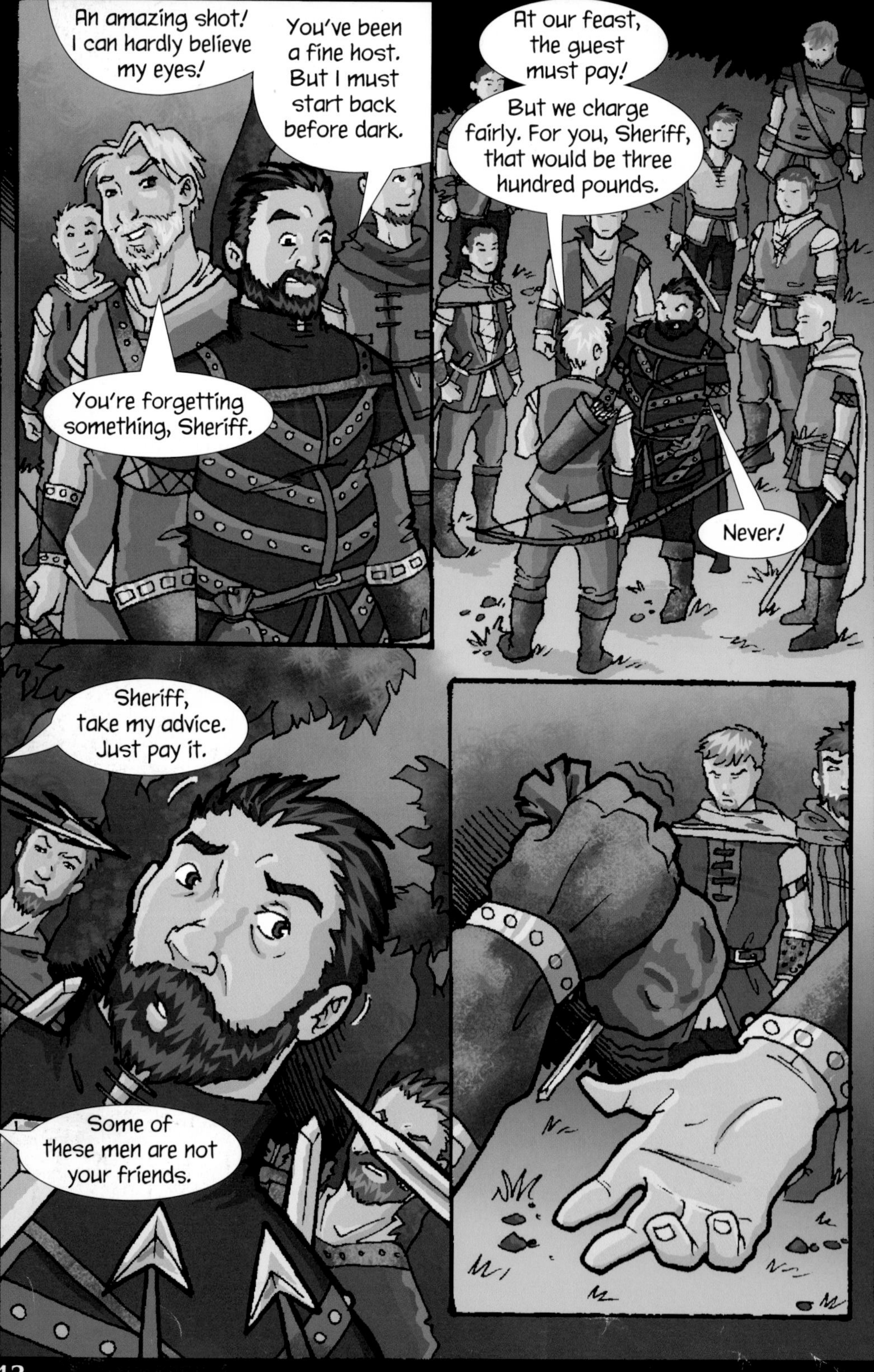
An amazing shot! I can hardly believe my eyes!
You've been a fine host. But I must start back before dark.
You're forgetting something, Sheriff.
At our feast, the guest must pay!
But we charge fairly. For you, Sheriff, that would be three hundred pounds.
Never!
Sheriff, take my advice. Just pay it.
Some of these men are not your friends.

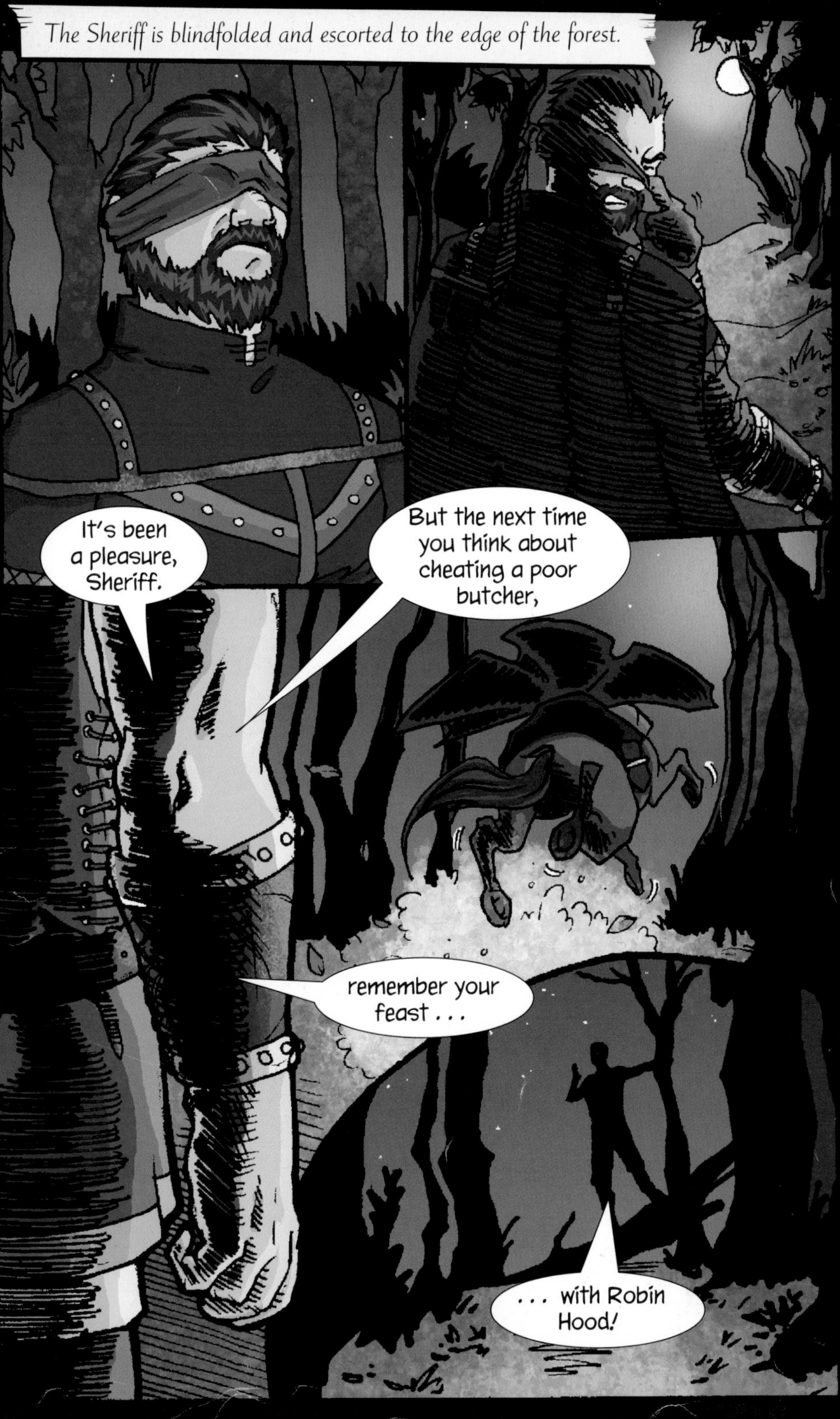
The Sheriff is blindfolded and escorted to the edge of the forest.
It's been a pleasure, Sheriff.
But the next time you think about cheating a poor butcher,
remember your feast . . .
. . . with Robin Hood!

Chapter 4 -The Final Contest

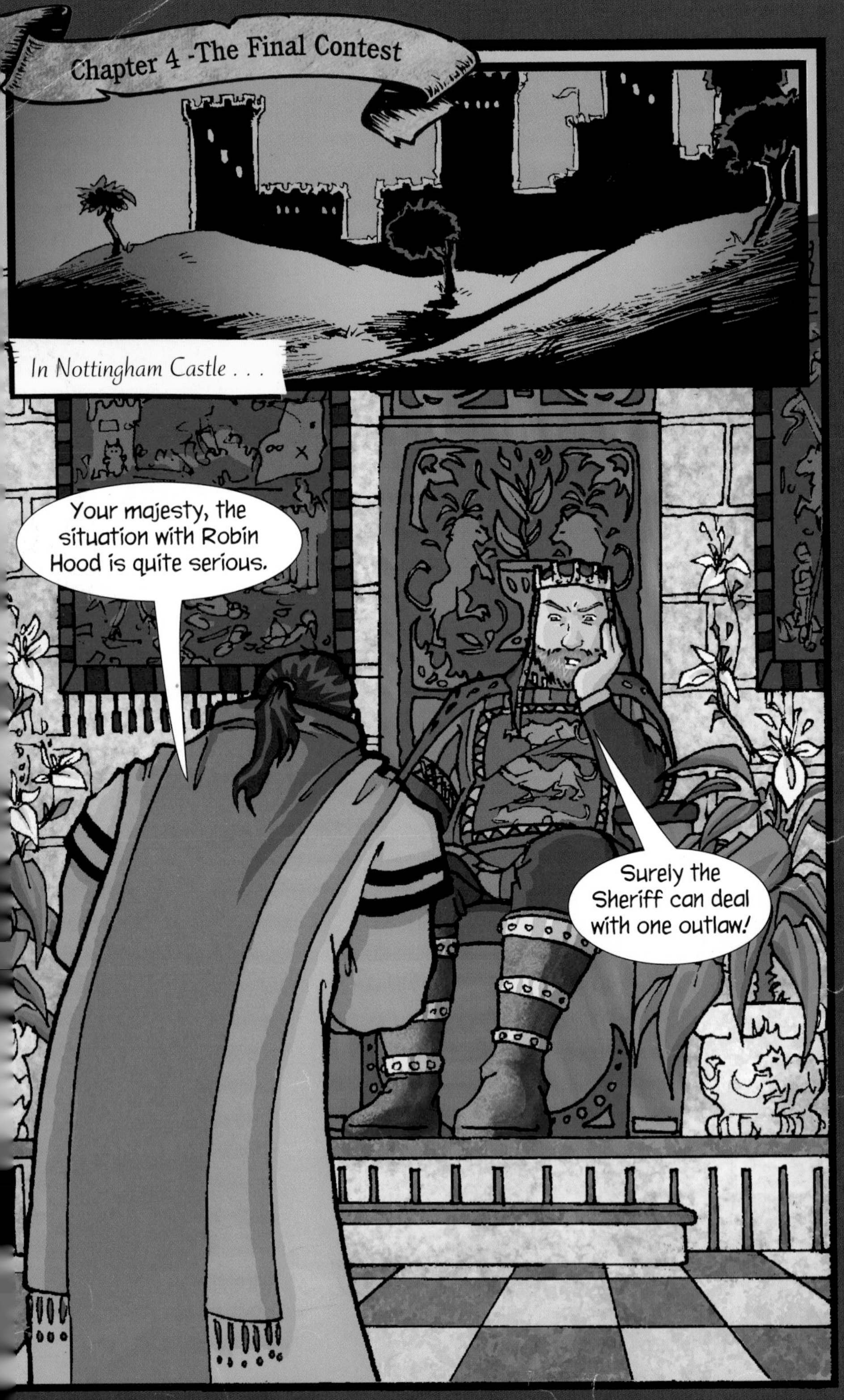
In Nottingham Castle . . .
Your majesty, the situation with Robin Hood is quite serious.
Surely the Sheriff can deal with one outlaw!

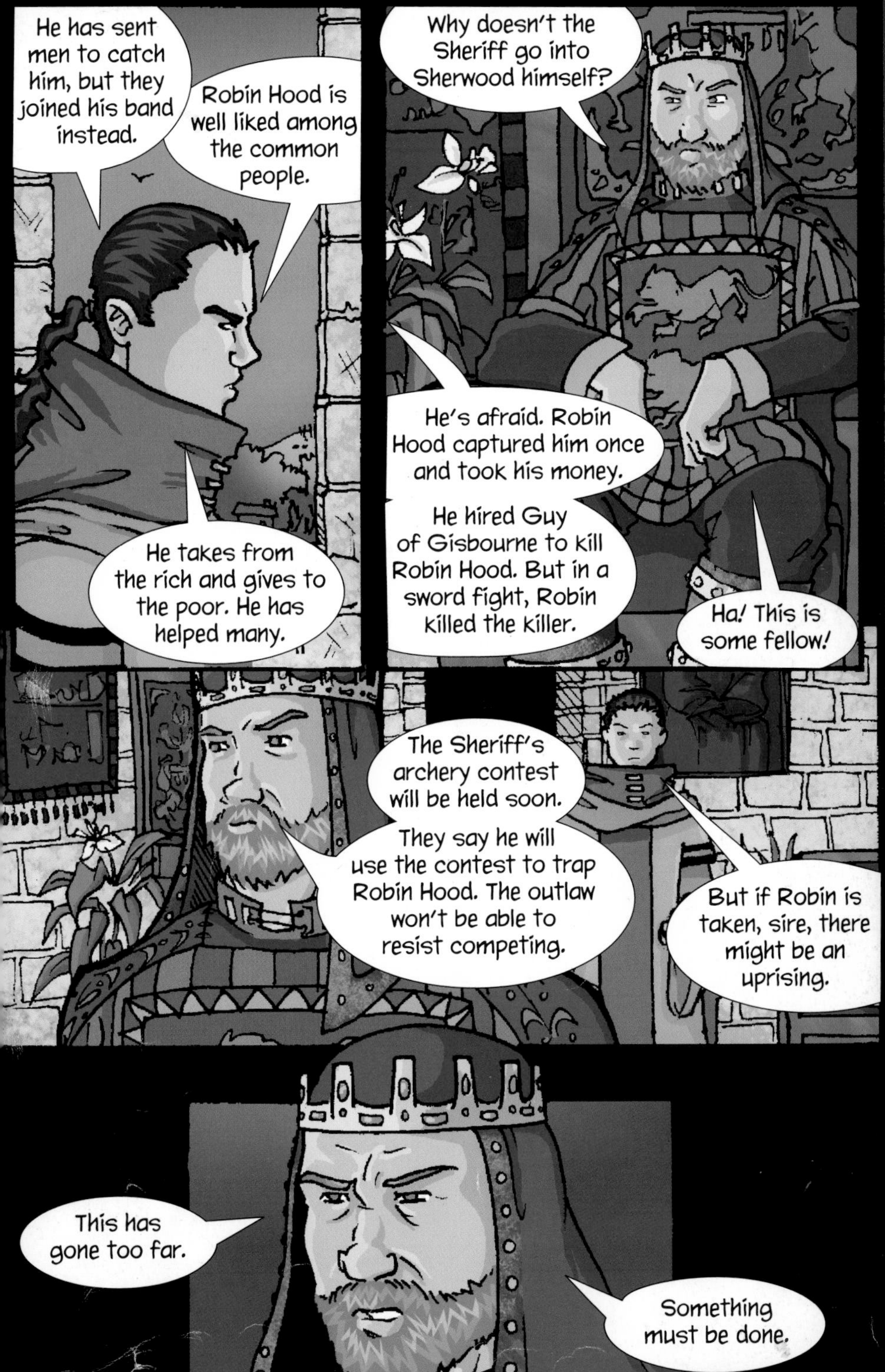
He has sent men to catch him, but they joined his band instead.
Robin Hood is well liked among the common people.
He takes from the rich and gives to the poor. He has helped many.
Why doesn't the Sheriff go into Sherwood himself?
He's afraid. Robin Hood captured him once and took his money.
He hired Guy of Gisbourne to kill Robin Hood. But in a sword fight, Robin killed the killer.
Ha! This is some fellow!
The Sheriff's archery contest will be held soon.
They say he will use the contest to trap Robin Hood. The outlaw won't be able to resist competing.
But if Robin is taken, sire, there might be an uprising.
This has gone too far.
Something must be done.

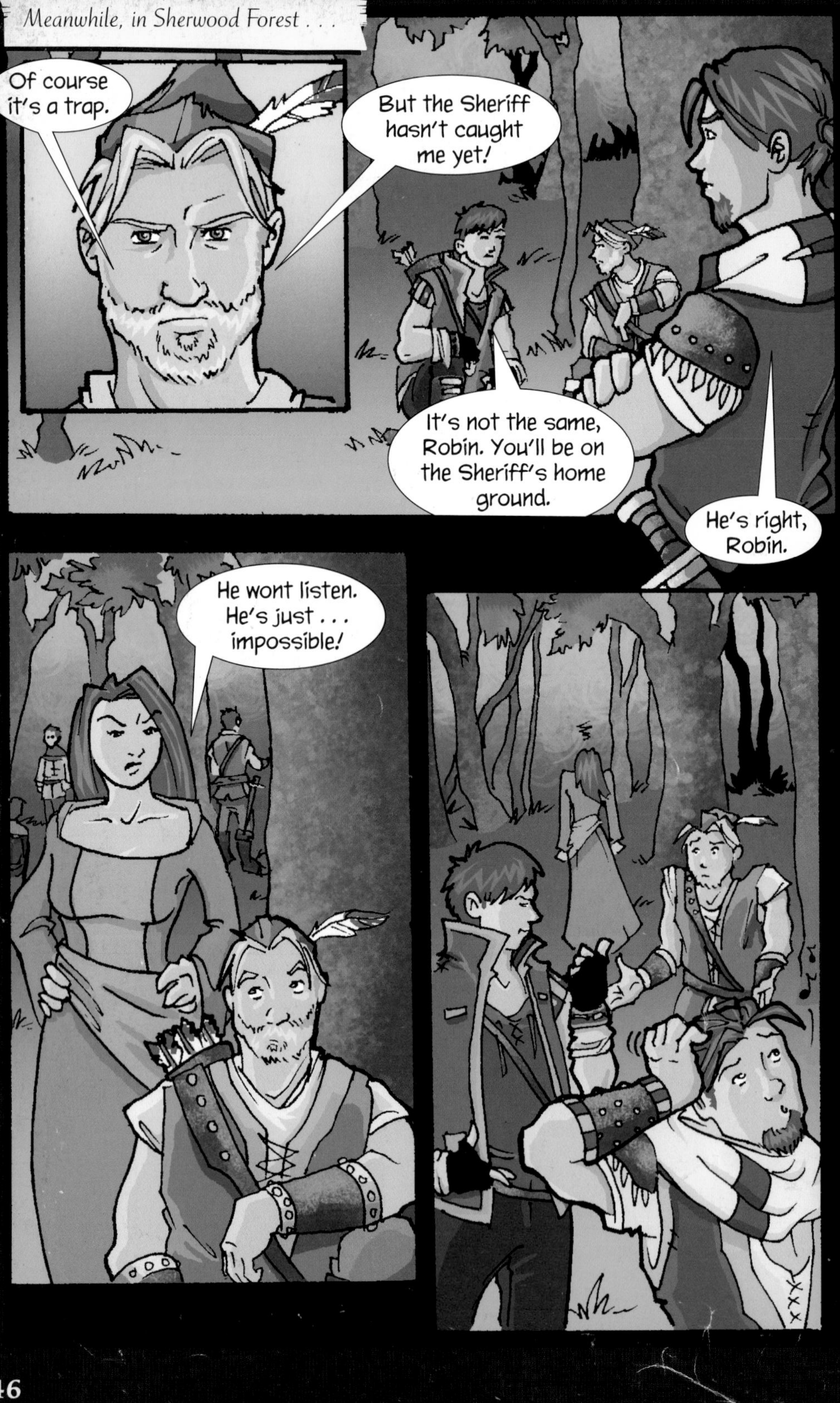
Meanwhile, in Sherwood Forest . . .
Of course it's a trap.
But the Sheriff hasn't caught me yet!
It's not the same, Robin. You'll be on the Sheriff's home ground.
He's right, Robin.
He wont listen. He's just . . . impossible!

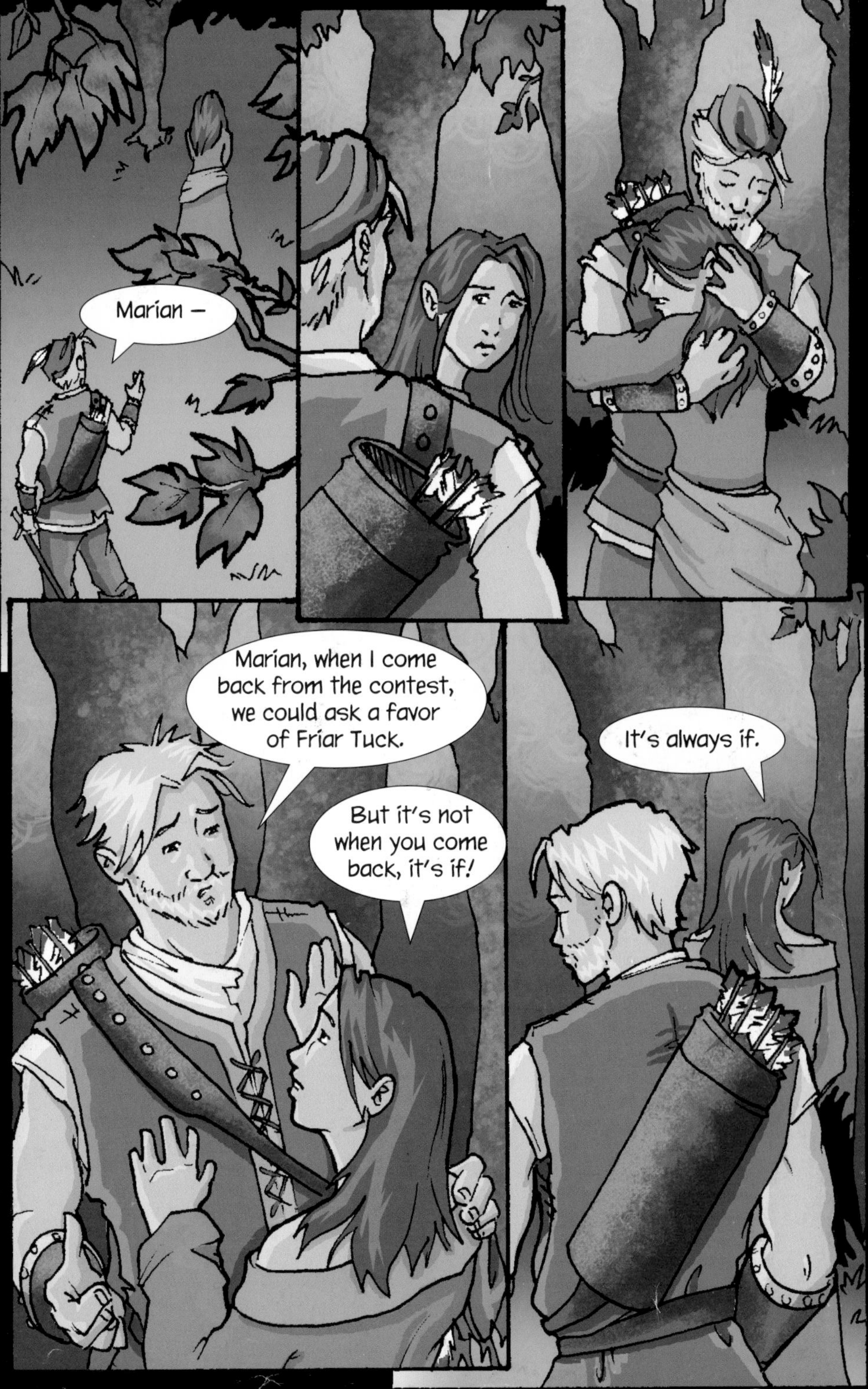
Marian –
Marian, when I come back from the contest, we could ask a favor of Friar Tuck.
But it's not when you come back, it's if!
It's always if.

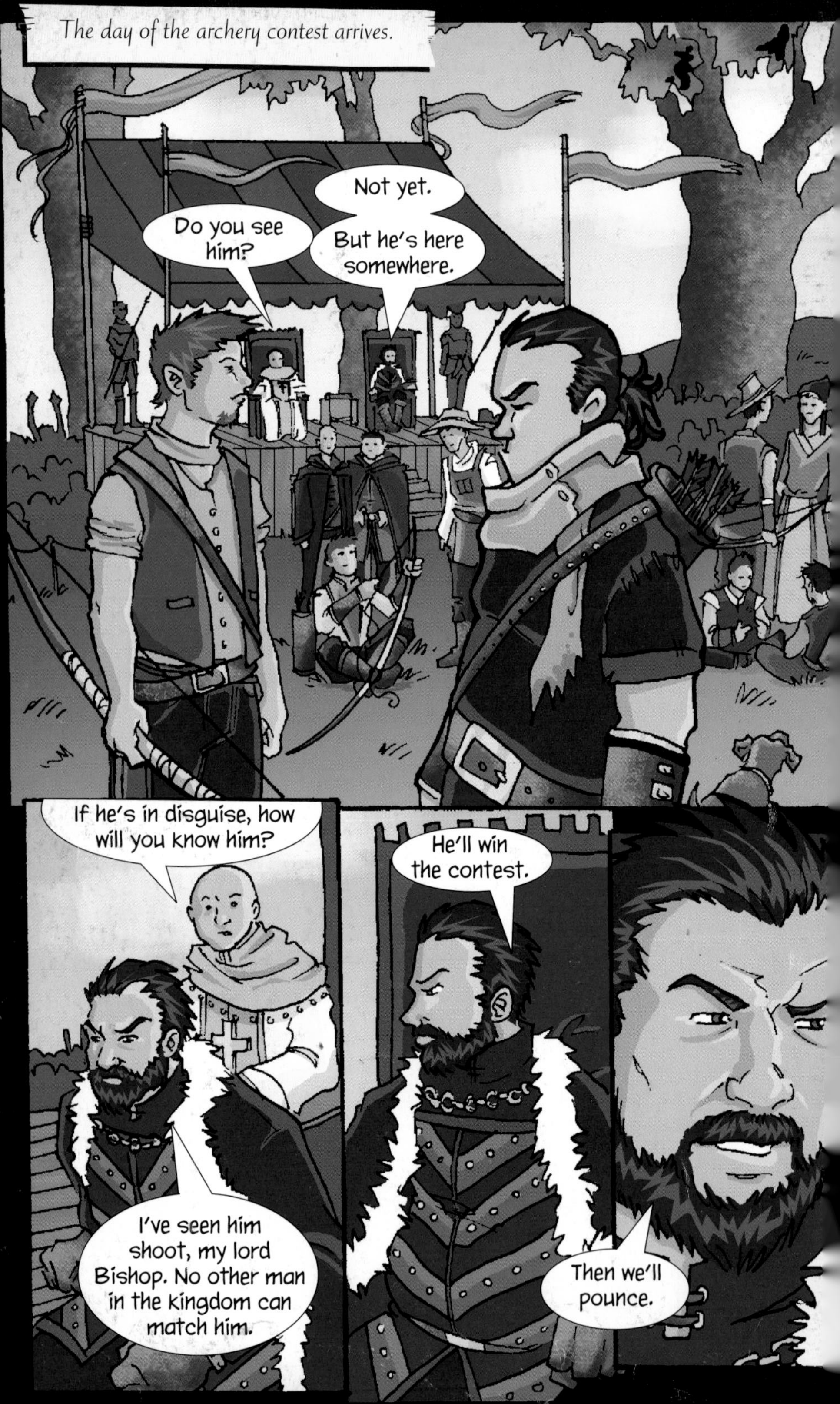
The day of the archery contest arrives.
Do you see him?
Not yet.
But he's here somewhere.
If he's in disguise, how will you know him?
I've seen him shoot, my lord Bishop. No other man in the kingdom can match him.
He'll win the contest.
Then we'll pounce.

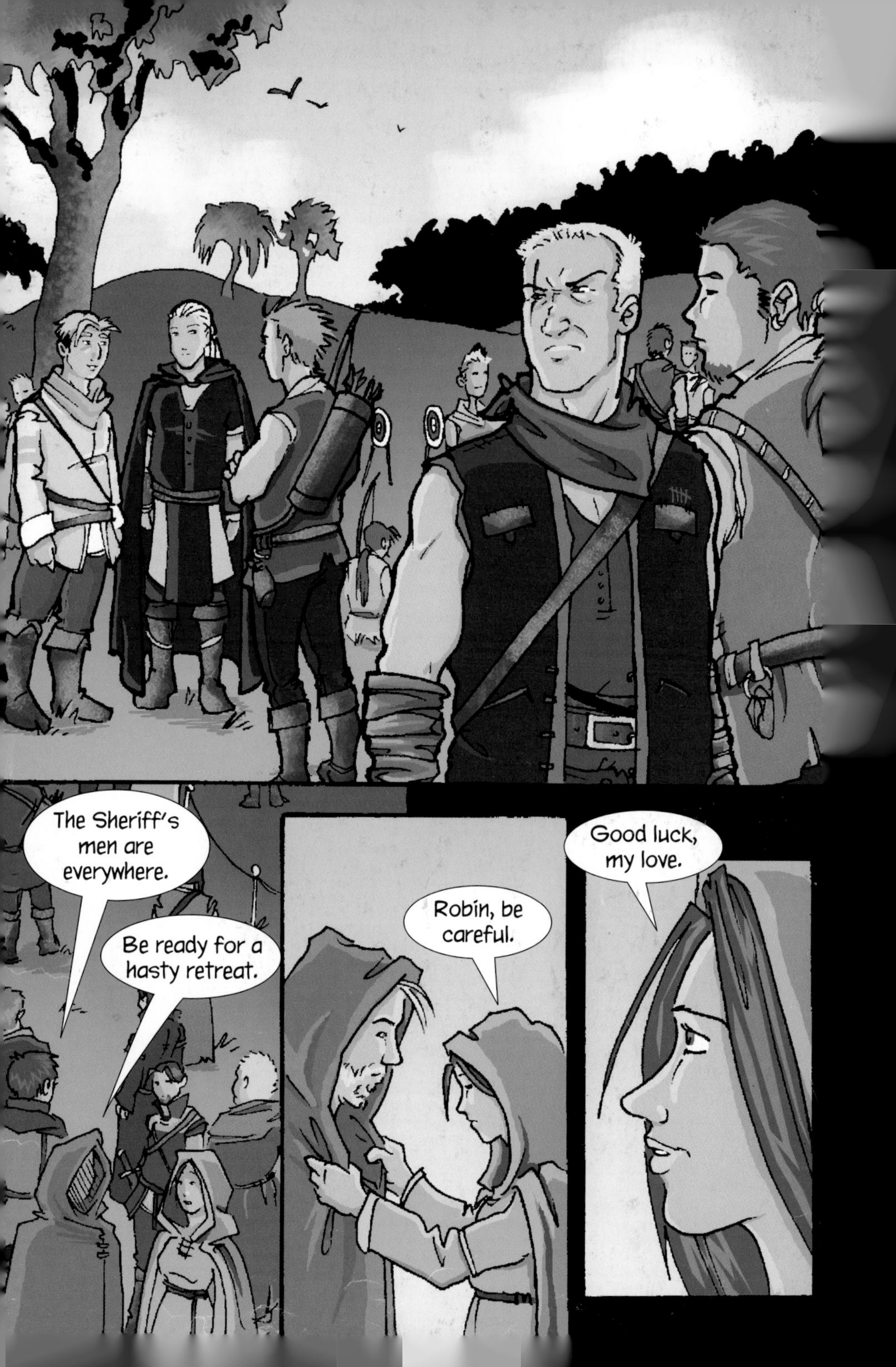
The Sheriff's men are everywhere.
Be ready for a hasty retreat.
Robin, be careful.
Good luck, my love.

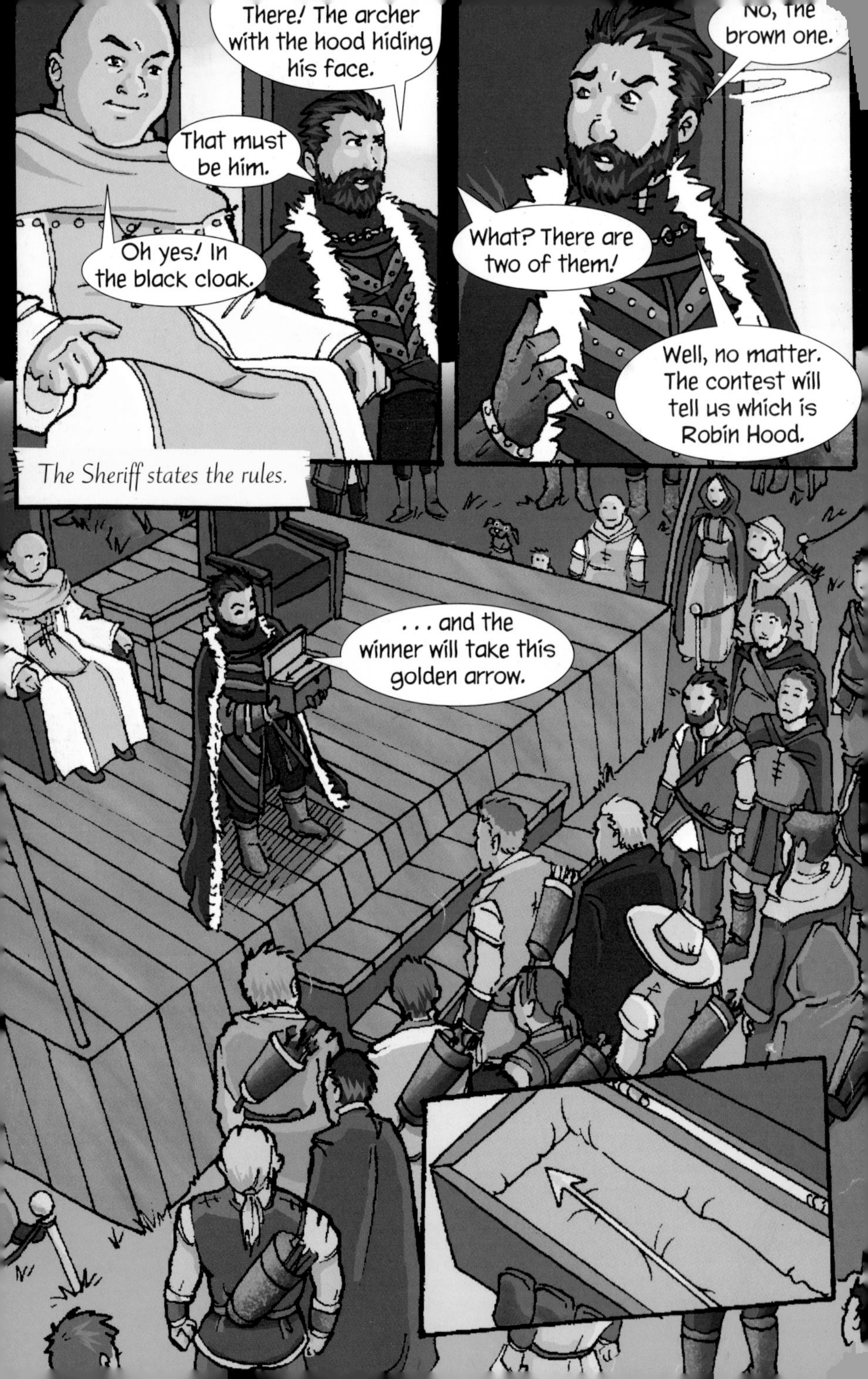
There! The archer with the hood hiding his face.
That must be him.
Oh yes! In the black cloak.
No, the brown one.
What? There are two of them!
Well, no matter. The contest will tell us which is Robin Hood.
The Sheriff states the rules.
. . . and the winner will take this golden arrow.

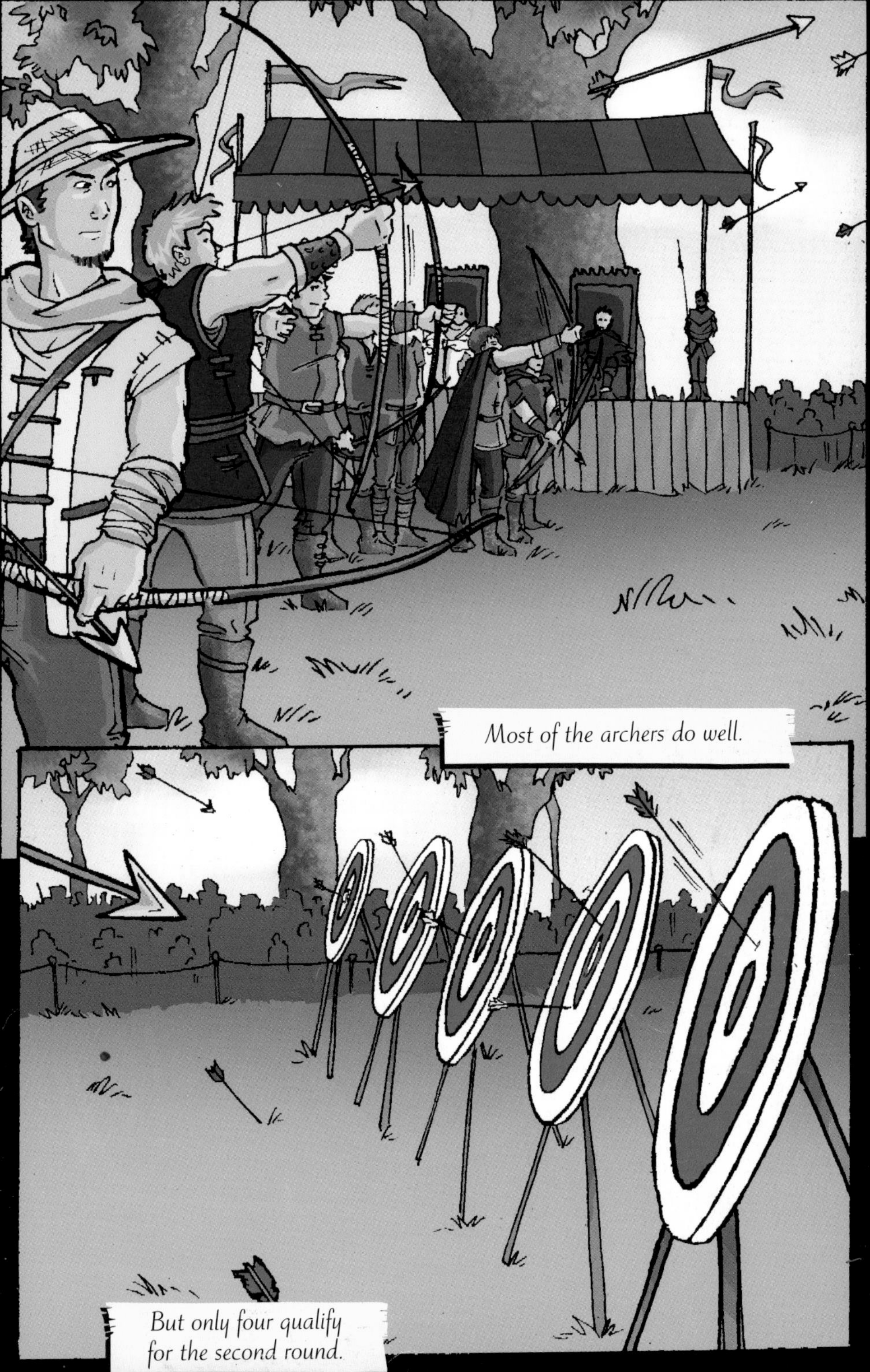
Most of the archers do well.
But only four qualify for the second round.

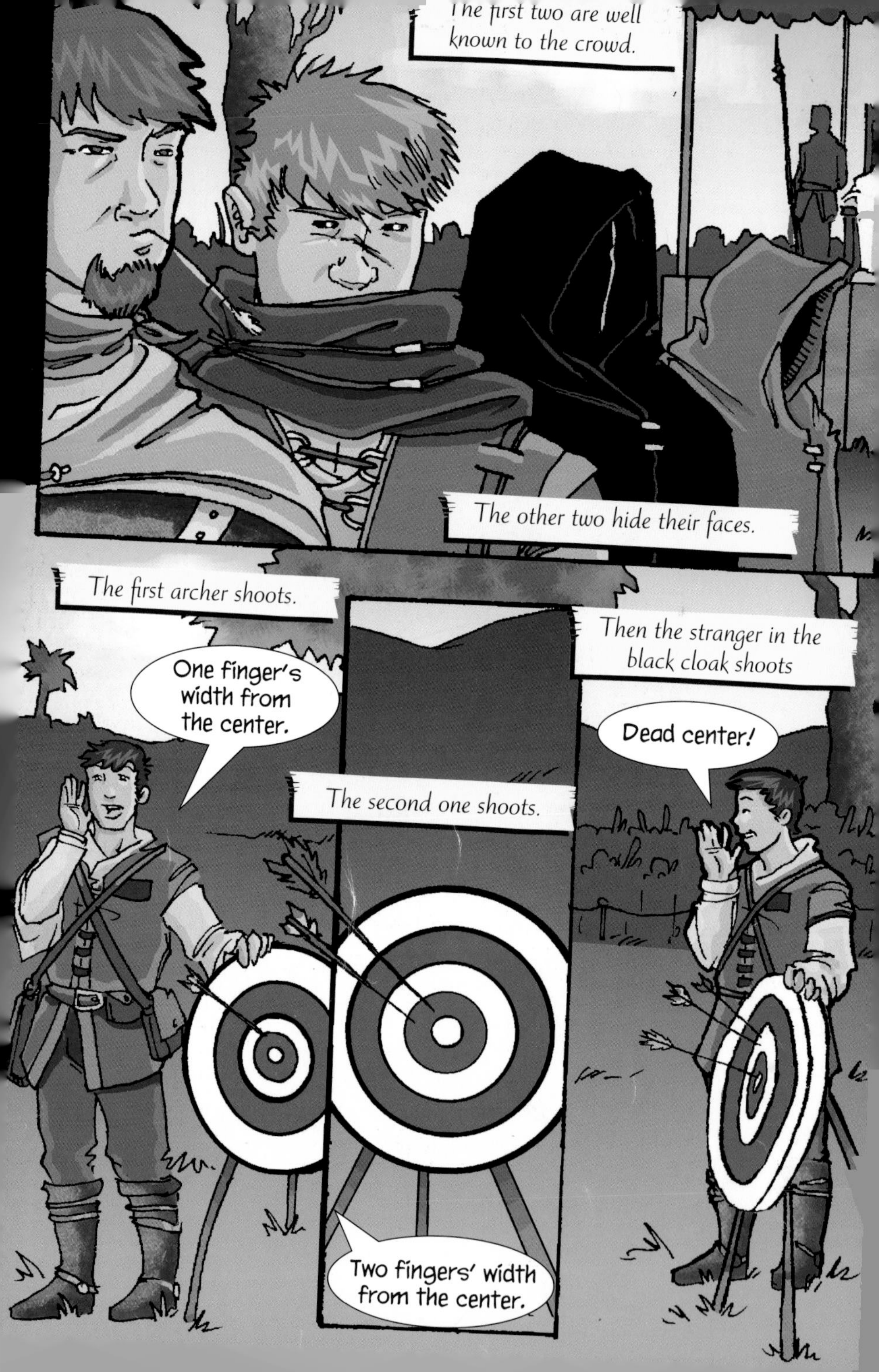
The first two are well known to the crowd.
The other two hide their faces.
The first archer shoots.
One finger's width from the center.
The second one shoots.
Two fingers' width from the center.
Then the stranger in the black cloak shoots
Dead center!

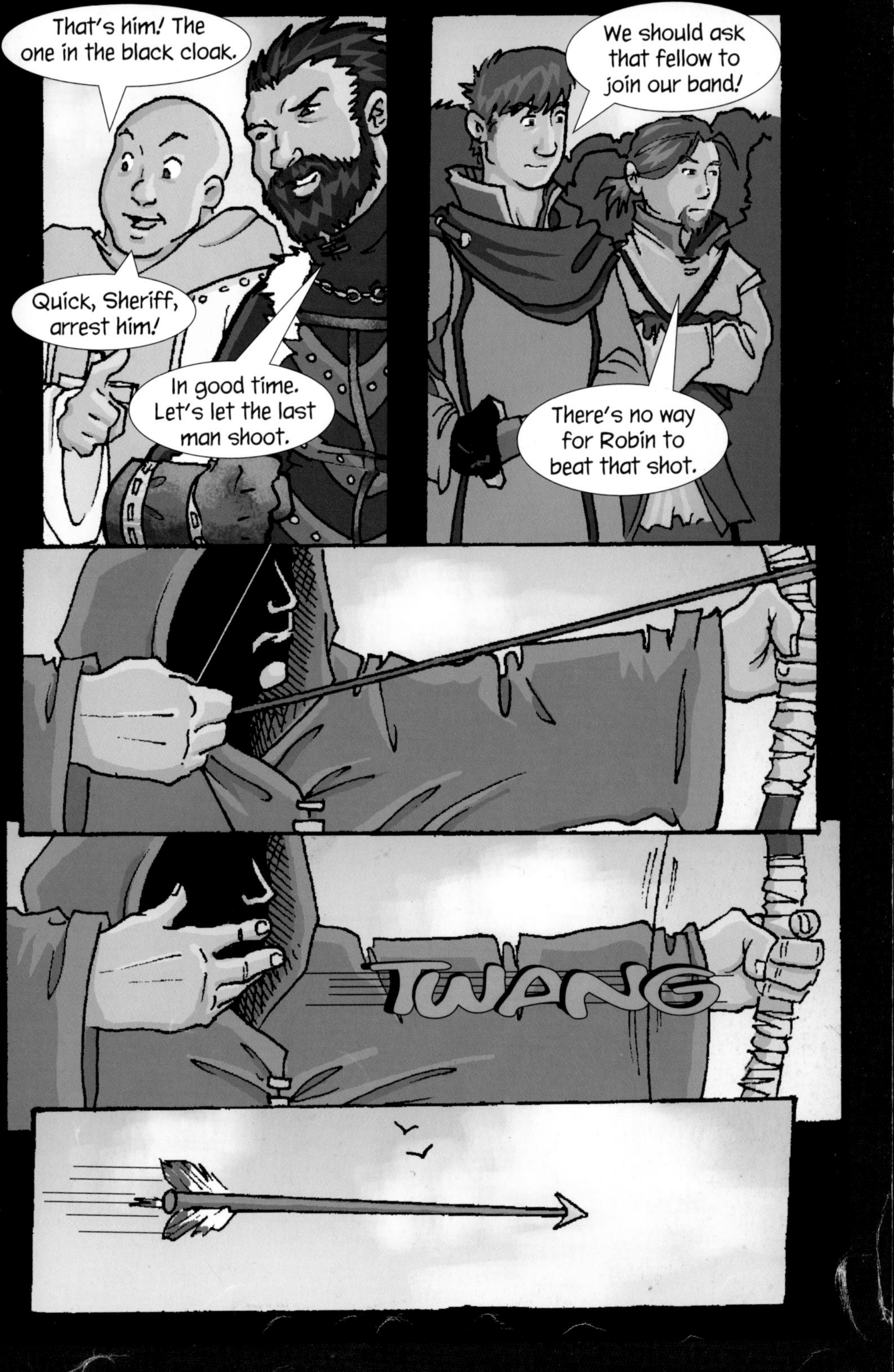
That's him! The one in the black cloak.
Quick, Sheriff, arrest him!
In good time. Let's let the last man shoot.
We should ask that fellow to join our band!
There's no way for Robin to beat that shot.
TWANG

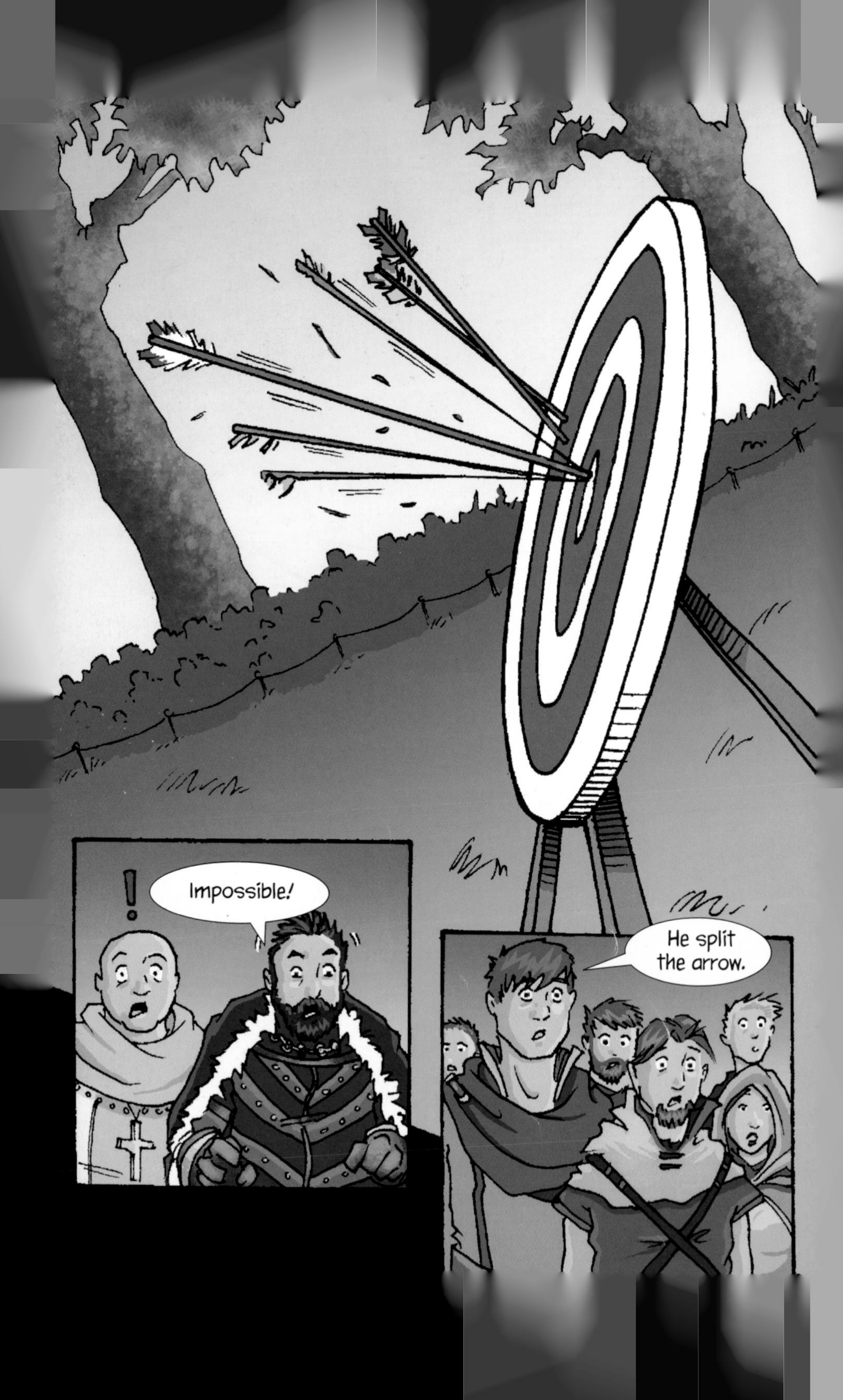
Impossible!
He split the arrow.

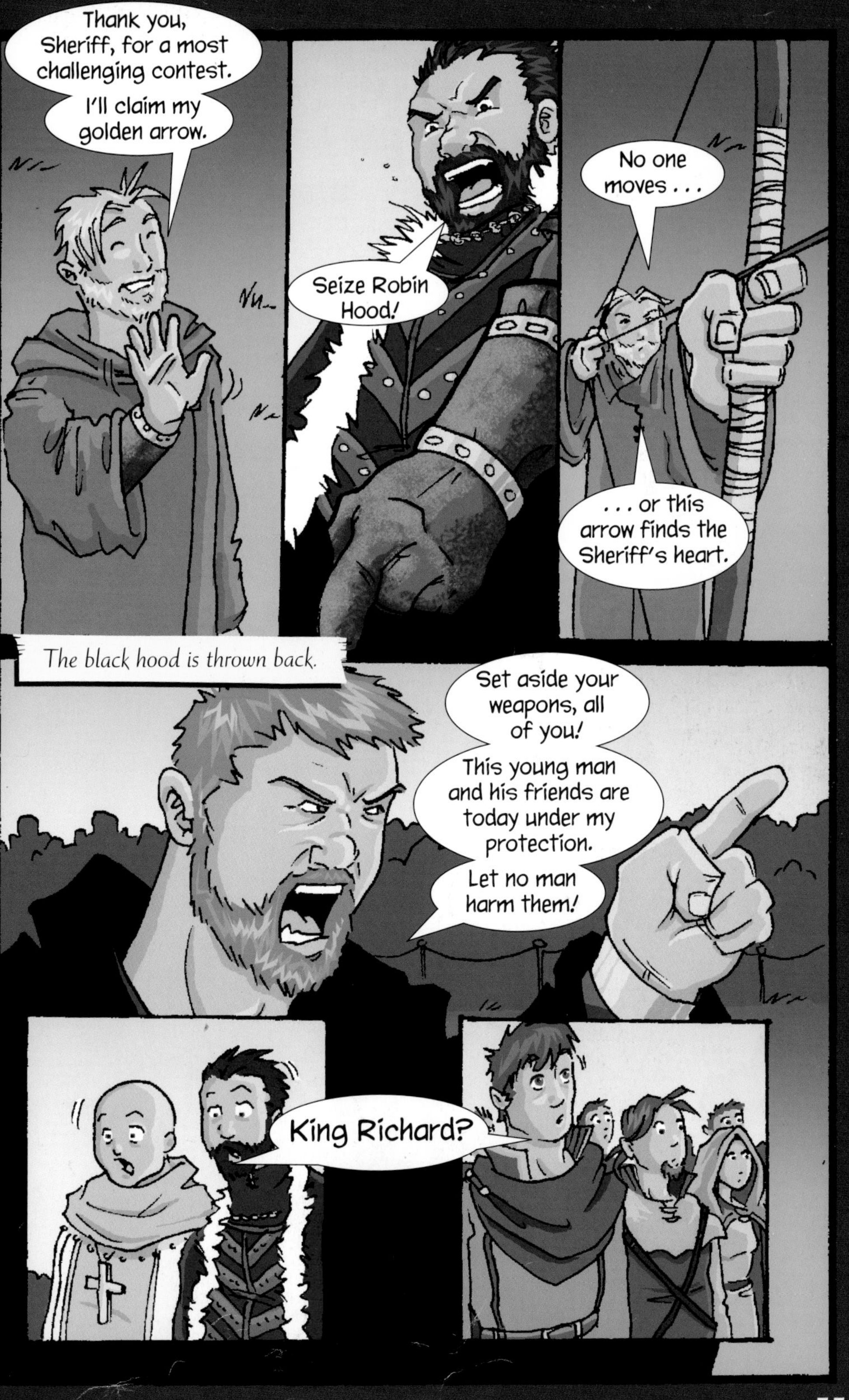

Thank you, Sheriff, for a most challenging contest.
I'll claim my golden arrow.
Seize Robin Hood!
No one moves . . .
. . . or this arrow finds the Sheriff's heart.
The black hood is thrown back.
Set aside your weapons, all of you!
This young man and his friends are today under my protection.
Let no man harm them!
King Richard?

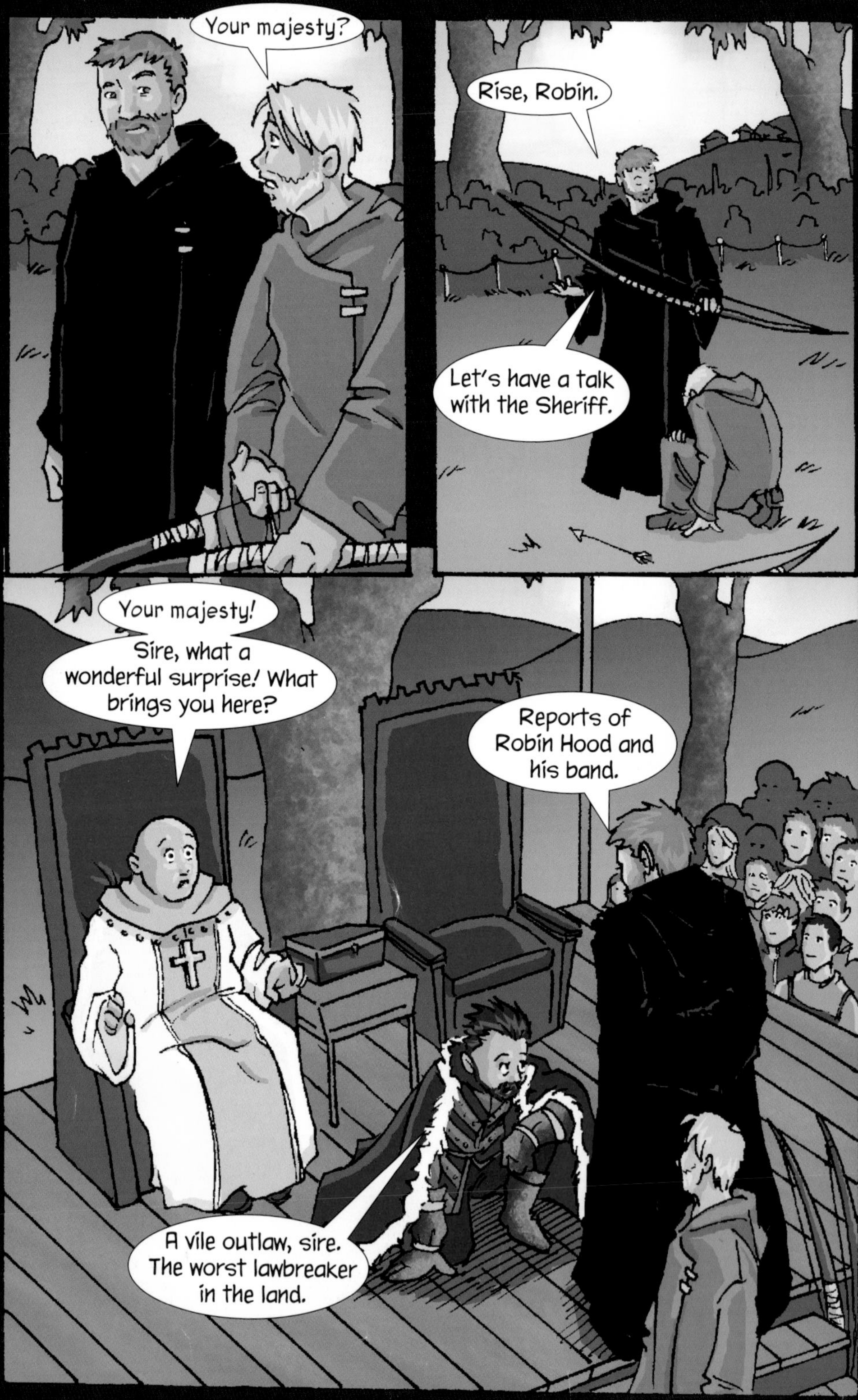

Your majesty?
Rise, Robin.
Let's have a talk with the Sheriff.
Your majesty!
Sire, what a wonderful surprise! What brings you here?
Reports of Robin Hood and his band.
A vile outlaw, sire. The worst lawbreaker in the land.

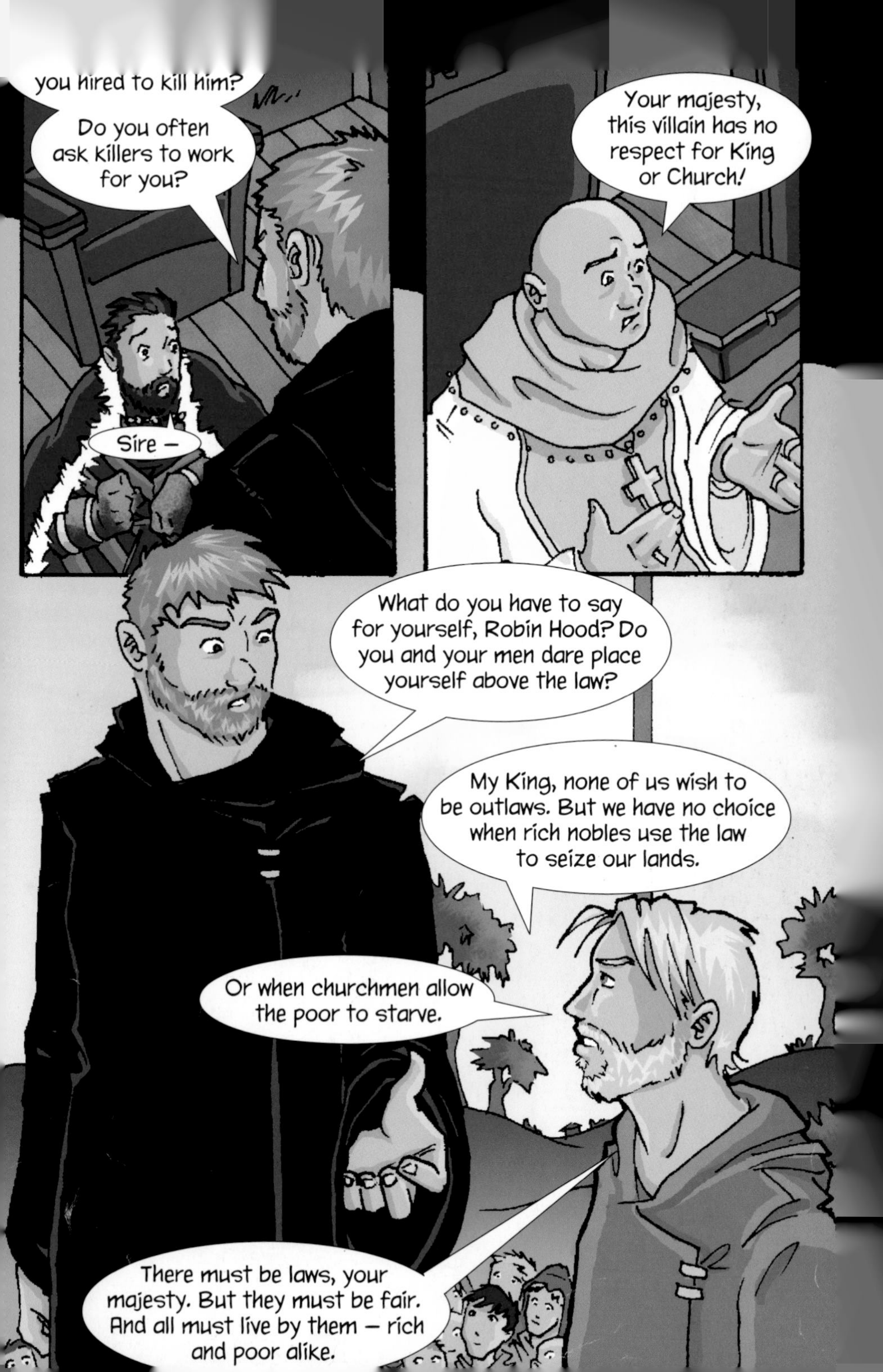

you hired to kill him?
Do you often ask killers to work for you?
Sire —
Your majesty, this villain has no respect for King or Church!
What do you have to say for yourself, Robin Hood? Do you and your men dare place yourself above the law?
My King, none of us wish to be outlaws. But we have no choice when rich nobles use the law to seize our lands.
Or when churchmen allow the poor to starve.
There must be laws, your majesty. But they must be fair. And all must live by them — rich and poor alike.

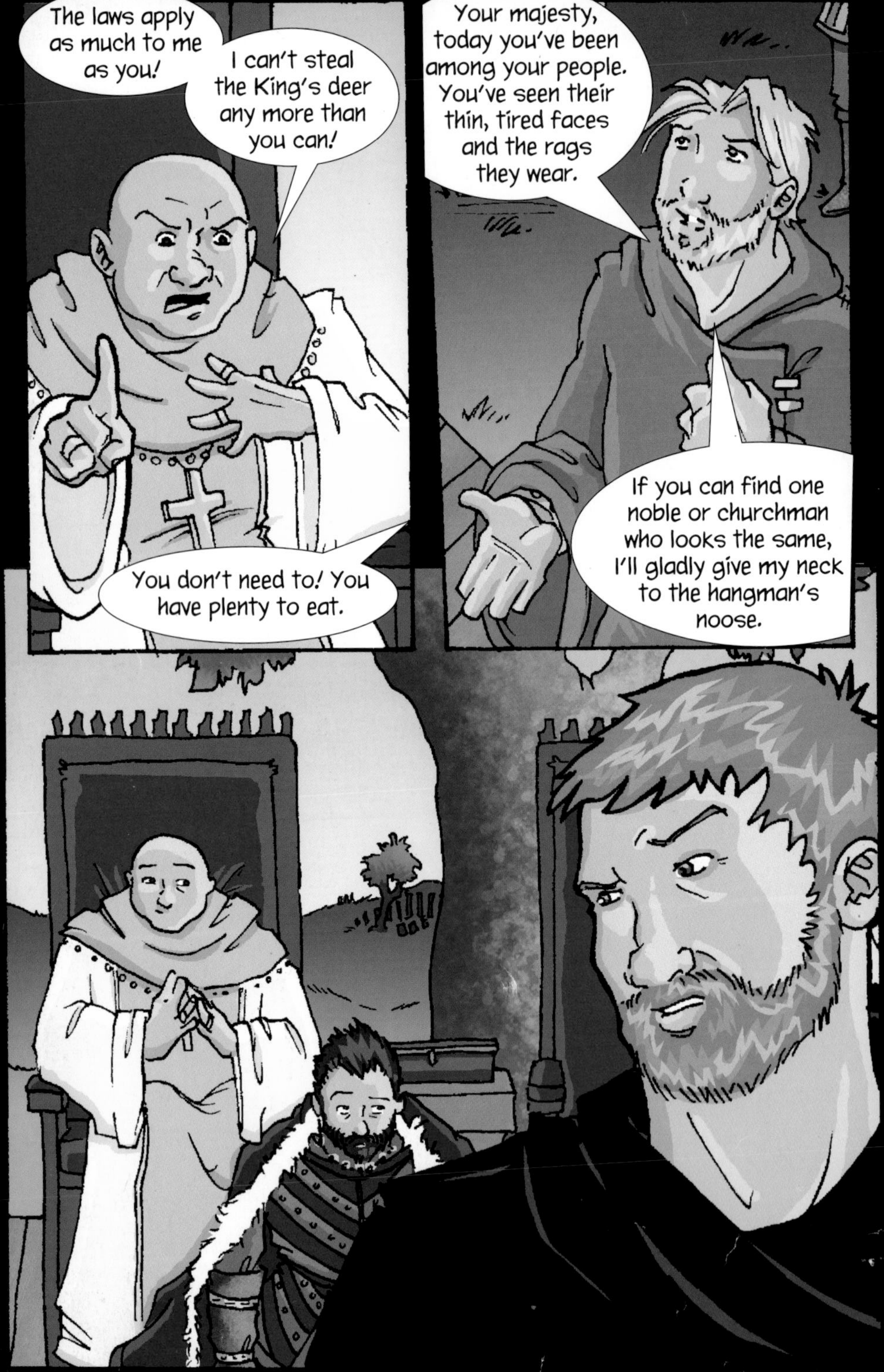
The laws apply as much to me as you!
I can't steal the King's deer any more than you can!
You don't need to! You have plenty to eat.
Your majesty, today you've been among your people. You've seen their thin, tired faces and the rags they wear.
If you can find one noble or churchman who looks the same, I'll gladly give my neck to the hangman's noose.

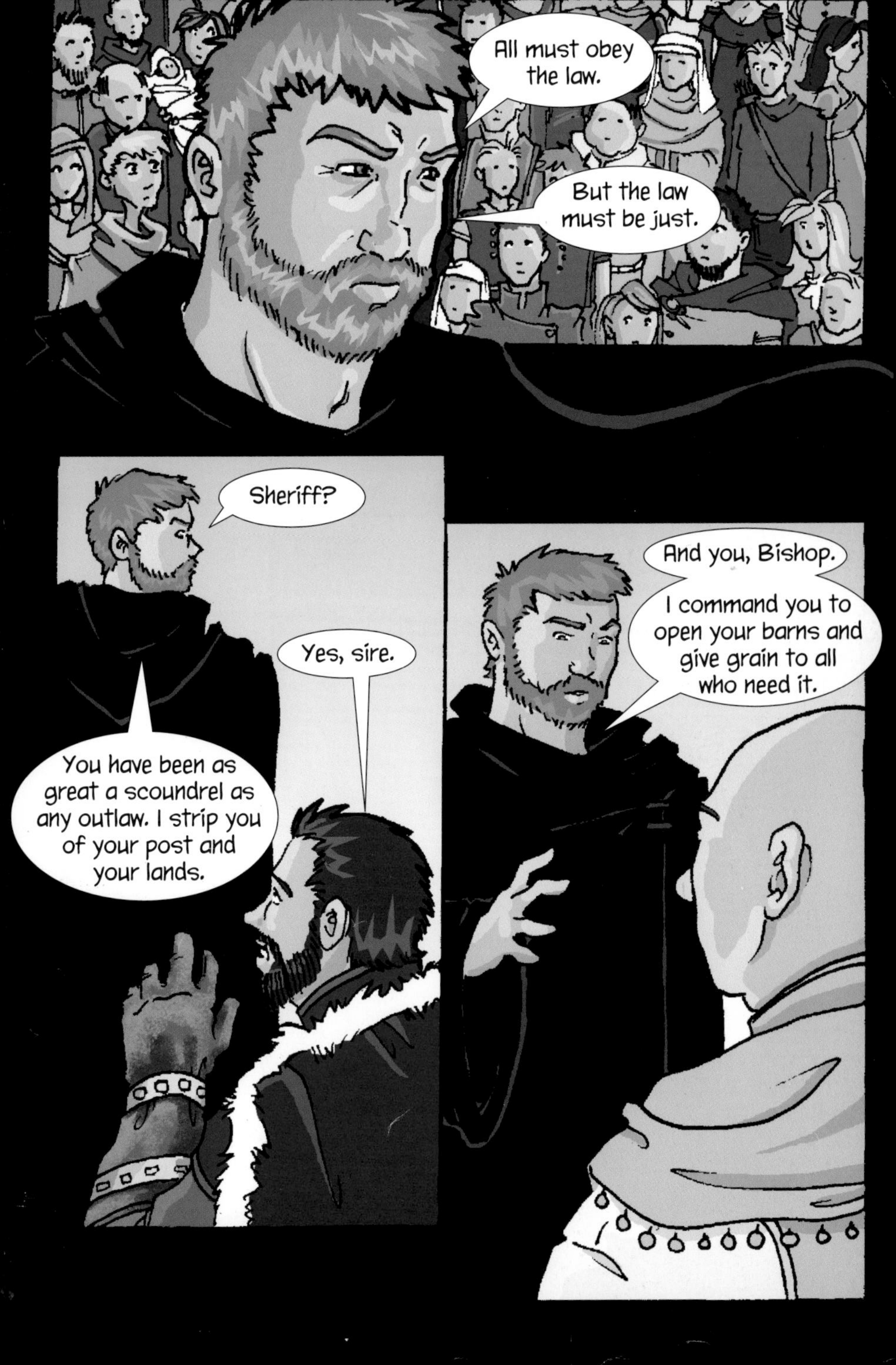

All must obey the law.
But the law must be just.
Sheriff?
You have been as great a scoundrel as any outlaw. I strip you of your post and your lands.
Yes, sire.
And you, Bishop.
I command you to open your barns and give grain to all who need it.

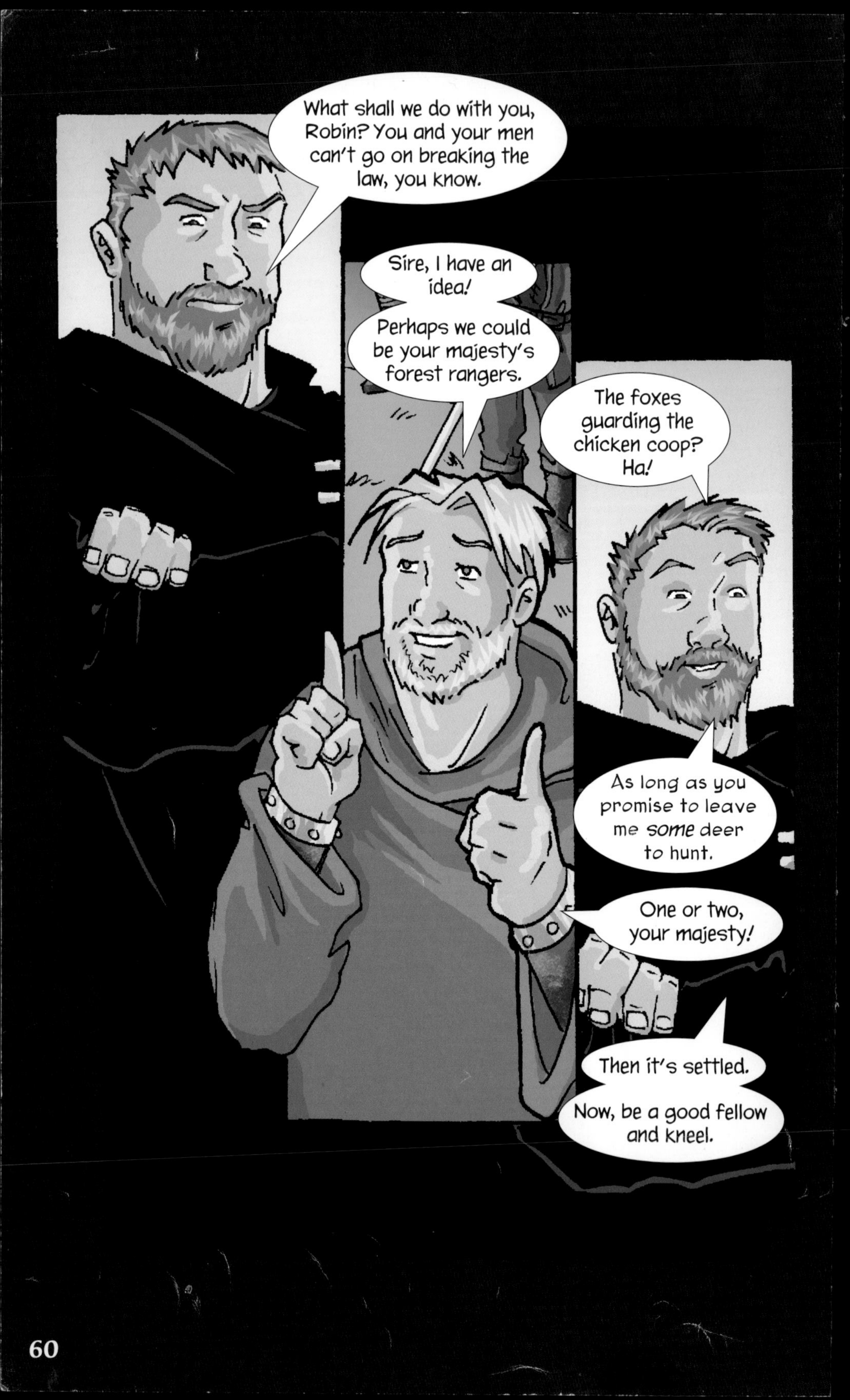
What shall we do with you, Robin? You and your men can't go on breaking the law, you know.
Sire, I have an idea!
Perhaps we could be your majesty's forest rangers.
The foxes guarding the chicken coop? Ha!
As long as you promise to leave me *some* deer to hunt.
One or two, your majesty!
Then it's settled.
Now, be a good fellow and kneel.

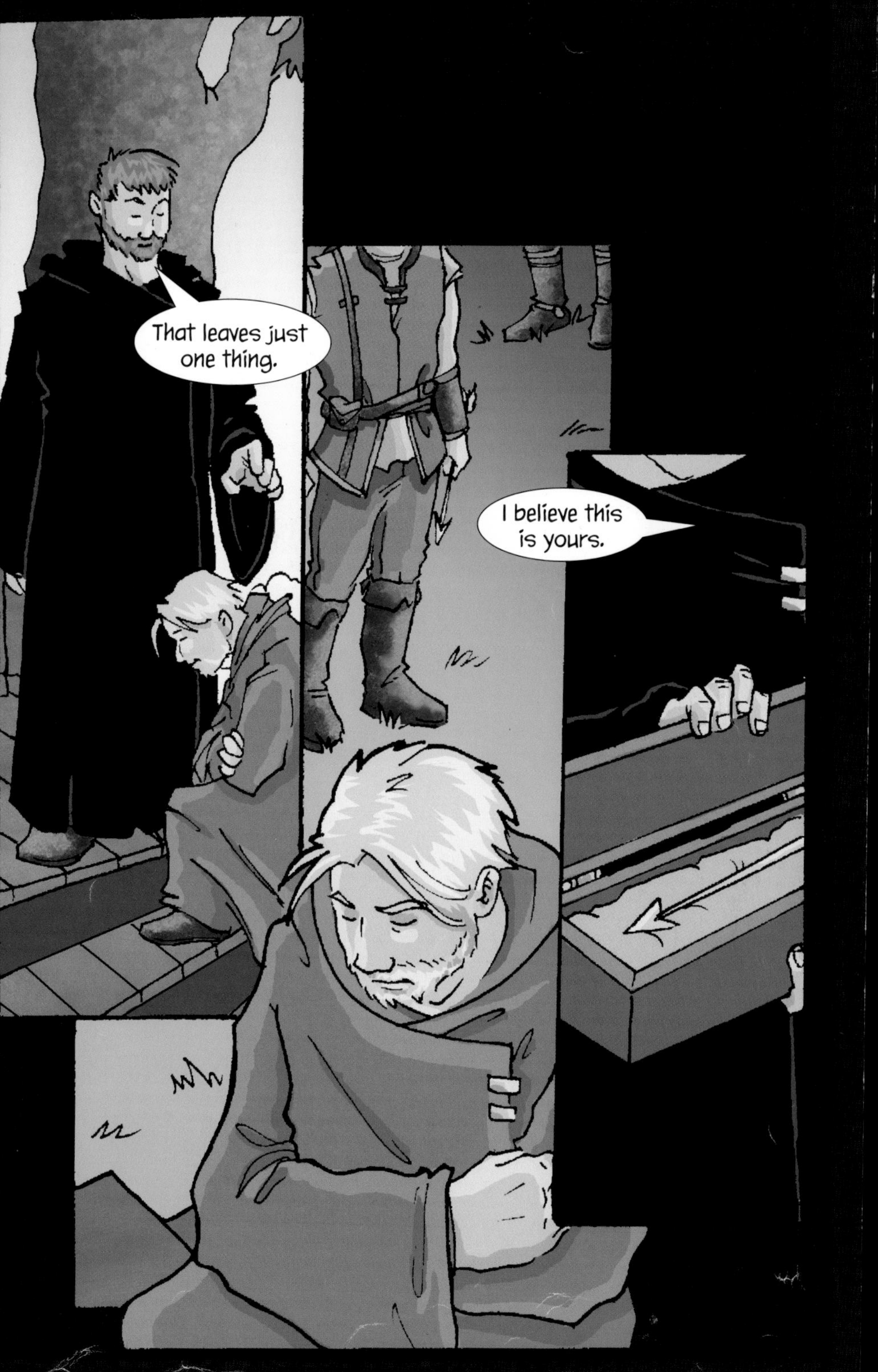
That leaves just one thing.
I believe this is yours.

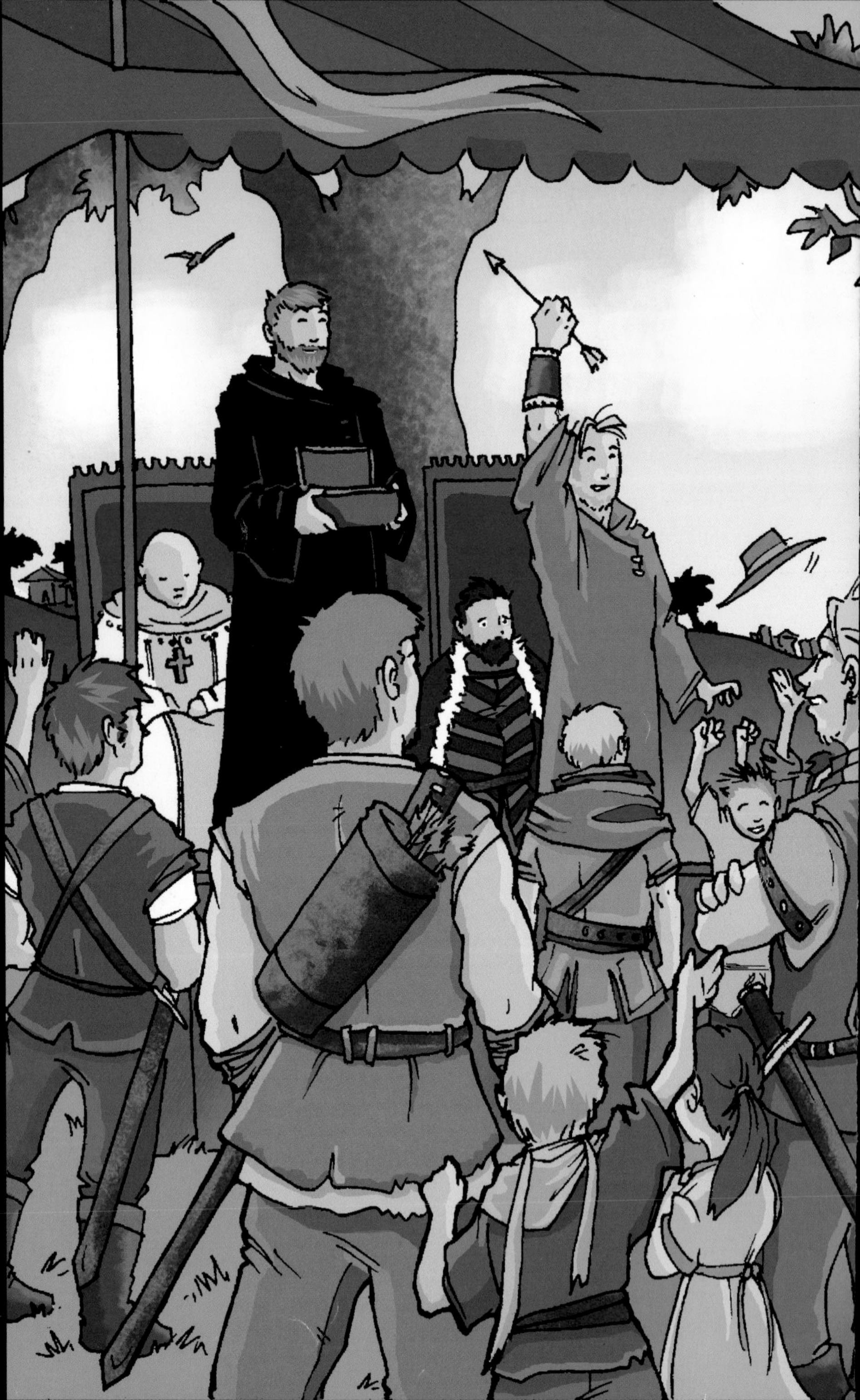

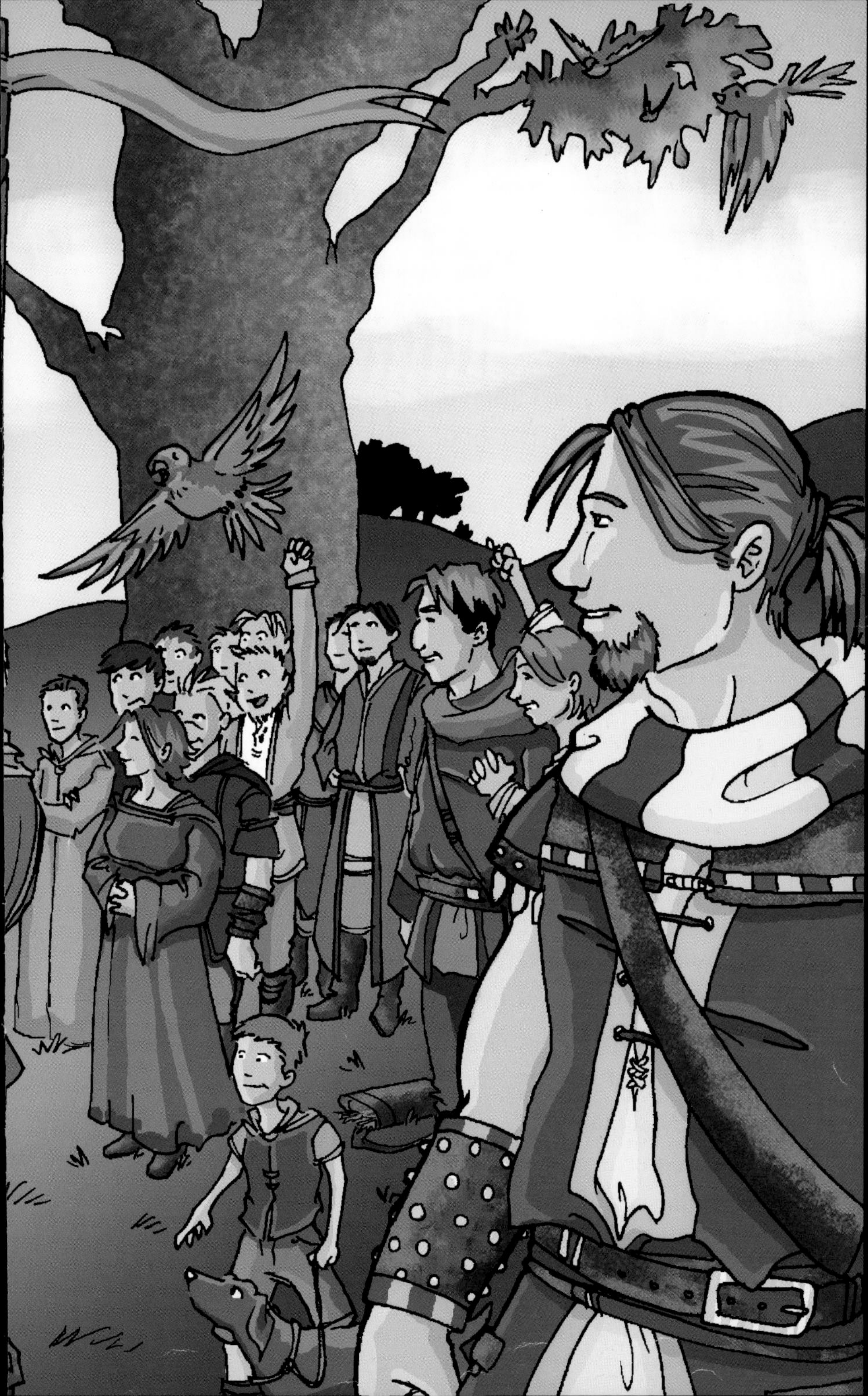

About Robin Hood

The stories of Robin Hood's adventures were first told hundreds of years ago in England. The earliest known written story, *The Gest of Robin Hood*, was written around 1500. The word "gest" means deed. This early version includes Maid Marian, Little John, and the Sheriff of Nottingham. In the 1800s, Howard Pyle, an American illustrator and writer, loved reading about Robin Hood. He retold these popular stories in 1883, in his book *The Merry Adventures of Robin Hood*.

About the Author

Aaron Shepard and Anne L. Watson are a husband and wife writing team. Aaron is the award-winning author of many retellings of folktales and world classics for young readers. His books include *The Legend of Lightning Larry* and *The Sea King's Daughter*. Anne is a novelist. They live in Olympia, Washington.

About the Illustrator

When she was young, Jennifer Tanner loved to draw humorous comics about dogs who went on spectacular adventures through time and space, meeting alien creatures along the way. She's never lost that love for telling stories with pictures. She attended the Savannah College of Art and Design where she received her degree in Sequential Art. Today she spends her time illustrating many comic books.

Glossary

abbey (AB-ee)—place where religious men and women live

archery (AR-chuh-ree)—a sport using a bow and arrows to hit a target

bishop (BISH-up)—the leader for churches in an area; the priests in the different churches report to the bishop

friar (FRY-ur)—a man whose job is to serve God and the church; monk is another name for a friar

groom (GROOM)—a man who is about to get married or was just married

minstrel (MIN-strul)—a person who works as a singer or plays a musical instrument

outlaw (OUT-law)—a person who disobeys the law and is in hiding

pound (POUND)—the English unit of money

staff (STAF)—a stick or cane used for walking

starving (STARV-ing)—dying because of a lack of food

tithe (TYTH)—part of a family's income or crop that the church collected to support its priests and bishops

Background of Robin Hood

Sherwood Forest, the setting for the tale of Robin Hood, is a forest that still exists in England. The forest today, however, is a much different place than it was in the late 1100s. Then, the forest belonged to the king of England. Only he and other noblemen were allowed to hunt there.

The sheriffs, friars, and bishops collected taxes and tithes from the people who lived in the communities near Sherwood Forest. Most of these people were poor farmers who worked hard to feed their families. These people relied on the goods of the forest — from the wood for heat and shelter to the plants and wildlife for food. Many people hunted illegally to provide their families with food, even though they could be hanged for breaking the law. Those who were in trouble with the law, like Robin Hood, often hid deep in the forest.

The story of Robin Hood, whether it was true or not, gave people hope that such an unfair way of living would come to an end.

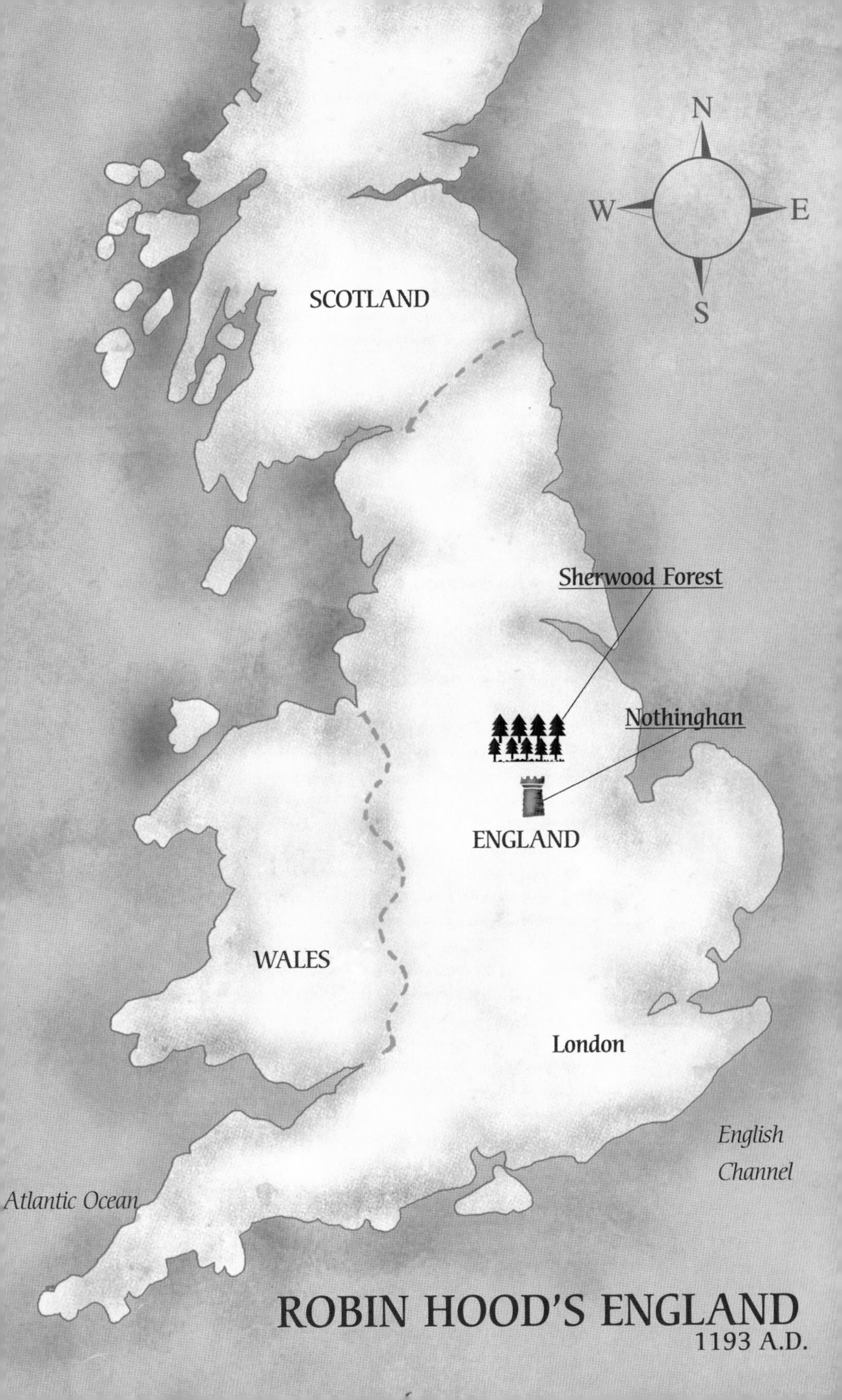

N
W
E
S
SCOTLAND
Sherwood Forest
Nothinghan
ENGLAND
WALES
London
English
Channel
Atlantic Ocean
ROBIN HOOD'S ENGLAND
1193 A.D.

Discussion Questions

1. Why did Robin Hood steal from the rich and give to the poor? Do you think that was fair? Why or why not?

2. Why did people join Robin Hood's band of thieves?

3. What if there were a person today who lived like Robin Hood, robbing rich people and giving the money to poor people. Would he be wanted by the police? Would his face be on the TV news? Would you want to join his band? Explain.

Writing Prompts

1. Instead of robbing from the rich, make a list of things you can actually do to help the poor in your community.

2. Robin Hood was very good at archery. Describe a sport or activity that you do well.

3. King Richard ruled over a kingdom that had very rich and very poor people living in it. If you were king or queen over a country like his, what would you do to make life more fair for everyone? Do you have ideas about how to be a good ruler?

Other Books

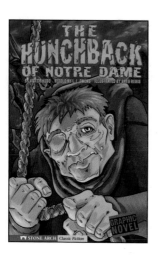

THE HUNCHBACK OF NOTRE DAME
GRAPHIC NOVEL
STONE ARCH Classic Fiction

THE HUNCHBACK OF NOTRE DAME

Hidden away in the bell tower of the Cathedral of Notre Dame, Quasimodo is treated like a beast. Although he is gentle and kind, he has the reputation of a frightening monster because of his physical deformities. He develops affection for Esmeralda, a gypsy girl who shows him kindness in return. When the girl is sentenced to an unfair death by hanging, Quasimodo is determined to save her. But those closest to Quasimodo have other plans for the gypsy.

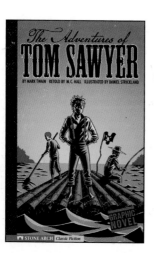

The Adventures of TOM SAWYER
BY MARK TWAIN RETOLD BY M.C. HALL ILLUSTRATED BY DANIEL STRICKLAND
GRAPHIC NOVEL
STONE ARCH Classic Fiction

THE ADVENTURES OF TOM SAWYER

Tom Sawyer is the cleverest of characters, constantly outwitting those around him. Then there is Huckleberry Finn, the envy of the town's schoolchildren because he has the rare gift of complete freedom, never attending school or answering to anyone but himself. After Tom and Huck witness a murder, they find themselves on a series of adventures that leads them to some seriously frightening situations.

Black
BEAUTY
GRAPHIC NOVEL
STONE ARCH Classic Fiction

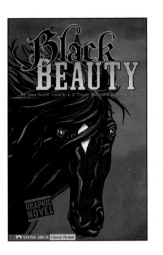

BLACK BEAUTY

Black Beauty, a handsome colt living in Victorian England, had a happy childhood growing up in the peaceful countryside. In his later years, he encounters terrible illness and a frightening stable fire. Things go from bad to worse when Black Beauty's new owners begin renting him out for profit. Black Beauty endures a life of mistreatment and disrespect in a world that shows little regard for the wellbeing of animals.

ROBERT LOUIS STEVENSON'S
TREASURE ISLAND
GRAPHIC NOVEL
STONE ARCH Classic Fiction

TREASURE ISLAND

Jim Hawkins had no idea what he was getting into when the pirate Billy Bones showed up at the doorstep of his mother's inn. When Billy dies suddenly, Jim is left to unlock his old sea chest, which reveals money, a journal, and a treasure map. Joined by a band of honorable men, Jim sets sail on a dangerous voyage to locate the loot on a faraway island. The violent sea is only one of the dangers they face. They soon encounter a band of bloodthirsty pirates determined to make the treasure their own!

Internet Sites

Do you want to know more about subjects related to this book? Or are you interested in learning about other topics? Then check out FactHound, a fun, easy way to find Internet sites.

Our investigative staff has already sniffed out great sites for you!

Here's how to use FactHound:

1. Visit *www.facthound.com*

2. Select your grade level.

3. To learn more about subjects related to this book, type in the book's ISBN number: **1598890492**.

4. Click the **Fetch It** button.

FactHound will fetch the best Internet sites for you!